Sarah Hall was born in C.... .. wice r.....
the ..... . the a.. .rd-v...., auth..
novels and three short-story collections: *The Beautiful Indifference*, which won the Edge Hill and Portico prizes, *Madame Zero*, winner of the East Anglian Book Award, and *Sudden Traveller*, shortlisted for the James Tait Black Prize for Fiction. She is currently the only author to be four times shortlisted for the BBC National Short Story Award, which she won in 2013 with 'Mrs Fox' and in 2020 with 'The Grotesques'.

Further praise for *Burntcoat*:

'A novel that feels more triggered by the pandemic than caused by it: visceral and intuitive, the prose is also non-stop glorious – a hymn to the physical and fragile nature of existence.' Anne Enright, *Irish Times*

'*Burntcoat* by Sarah Hall is in the vanguard of a new genre of pandemic/lockdown fiction: the connections between isolation and creation are laid bar.... of the not-quite-now.' Damon Ga....

'An elemental novel.' *Financial T....*

'A bravura exploration of art, love, sex and ego.' Justine Jordan, *Guardian*

'From award-winning and Booker Prize-nominated writer Sarah Hall comes this intense, almost claustrophobic, but compelling story about life, death, love, longing – all the big themes deftly and beautifully explored.' Sarra Manning, *Red*

'Sarah Hall has always written about the unsettling edges of life – eerie landscapes, animalistic desires – so the pandemic was a perfect crucible for *Burntcoat*, her sixth novel, and one of the books of the year so far.' Cal Revely-Calder, *Daily Telegraph*

'Hall skilfully probes the way that confined existence exacerbates existing wounds to the psyche. *Burntcoat* is a beguiling tale about our unending struggle to work out how to exist and how to learn to live with loss.' Martin Chilton, *Independent*

'An elemental novel, of earth and fire and water, wood and mud and peat, graphite and charcoal, resins, pine tar and ashes . . . woven from the English landscape . . . This is fertile territory for Hall, whose previous work has so brilliantly sung of the north.' Lauren Elkin, *Financial Times*

'Beguiling . . . Hall writes in exquisite prose about desire and death in the midst of a national crisis.' Anita Sethi, *Vogue*

'An extraordinary book . . . Her writing is subtle, richly textured, requiring time to give it the full attention it needs and to savour its beauty.' Susan Osborne, A Life in Books

BURNTCOAT

○

SARAH HALL

faber

First published in 2021
by Faber & Faber Limited
74–77 Great Russell Street
London WC1B 3DA

This paperback edition first published in 2022

Typeset by Typo•glyphix, Burton-on-Trent DE14 3HE
Printed and bound in England by CPI Group (UK) Ltd,
Croydon CRO 4YY

The poem 'Keep the Change' by Cemal Süreya, translated into English
by Hamit Sert and Sarah Hall. Reproduced by permission of the estate
of the author through Can Publishing

A CIP record for this book is available from the British Library

ISBN 978–0–571–32934–2

2 4 6 8 10 9 7 5 3 1

For my daughter and my father

BURNTCOAT

Those who tell stories survive.

My mother said this to me when I was a child, after she'd gone missing for several hours. I was convinced she was dead and that I'd been left alone in the cottage on the moors. When she arrived home, soaked and coatless in the dark, she didn't understand why I was crying. She'd been out walking and had lost track of time.

What would I do alone? I shouted at her. *I can't look after myself.*

It wasn't true, of course – I could make a fire and use the oven; by the age of ten I could drive her car. I was ready for her to disappear.

Naomi looked at my wet, distressed face. Her own was expressionless. She shrugged. *Those who tell stories survive,* she said, as if issuing literal advice.

Naomi had a habit of mixing up words and ideas, and I thought she was confused or meant the reverse – survivors tell stories. I tried to correct her but she insisted.

Thank you, Edith – I can stand.

This was her customary phrase, code for resumed authority over me, and not meant unkindly. At that point she'd not written a book for several years, her workshops brought in very little money and we were struggling. Lofty, baroque hair had grown over the tracks in her scalp. Looking at her, no one would've known she had relearnt everything, including how to speak, how to write her name. She'd survived – catastrophic war inside her brain and reconstruction outside.

I've thought about what she meant. Is it possible to be saved, like Scheherazade seducing the enemy with tales? Do stories make sense of a disordered world? Perhaps Naomi was saying that life is only an invention, a version necessary for us to accept living.

Today I prepared my bed. New sheets stretched tight across the mattress, the smell of air and sunshine on them from drying in the yard, blossom in the creases. Spring again – it seems to be the human weak point, when we're tired after winter, beginning to loosen our grip and imagine escape. I remember a saying from your country – in spring, don't burn the handle of the axe. I've made soup and some soft dishes, enough for a week or so. A few books are on the table, including Naomi's, and a volume of translated poetry. This time of year the angle of light on the river changes, slanting up the walls and in through the bedroom window. The studio below is lit like a bulb.

There's still time to organise, but most things are done. Tomorrow I will go to the market, to the flower stall. I'm sure Rostam will find what I want without getting sentimental. I haven't tidied. We are who we are, there's little point pretending otherwise. The apartment doesn't contain much anyway, and in the studio the last piece is finished, lying disassembled, ready to mount. My installer has been over the designs and the maquette many times, made the calculations and steel armature. It's too big to try raising inside, even though the ceiling is high. I trust Sean. He knows the direction it should face – east, with the wind behind the rotor – the weight and sail of the structure, the wood's liable twist and settle once it's outside. Strange to think I won't see it in location on the memorial hill. The truth is, I have trouble even looking at it now. There have been times I've covered the lovers' faces with tarpaulin. Times when I could have taken a hammer and torch to them.

Karolina has held off the project for years – decades. She's long past retirement and keeps few clients; I'm lucky she's loyal. This commission is the bane of her life. All the hidden costs and the delays. No doubt there will be controversy when it finally goes up, and Sir Philip will regret his decision. But I won't have to deal with the fallout.

There's no one to inherit so I've made provision for Burntcoat to pass over to The Heritage. The machinery alone is worth thousands, and the Bullfinches are in good condition; they could be used by roofers. Perhaps they will open the workroom again, let people come in and watch. There are keys with the solicitor and I will post a set to Karolina along with the letter of instruction. I'm sure she's imagined the scenario. The exterior walls, specifically the words painted on them, aren't to be touched. I don't want a plaque.

I should call the medical centre, but haven't been there in years – I was sick of the tests and the questions, so many vials of blood, being told there was no physical damage, or neurodivergence, being told I was traumatised, then that I was remarkable. I don't know the names of any of the doctors, and I don't want assistance. I still get letters to attend nova clinics – they aren't called that any more – but I've passed so many markers, and I'm not monitored now. Fifty-nine is old for carriers.

I thought at first it was tiredness, the aftermath of a particularly hard winter. Burntcoat is like a cathedral, vaulted, difficult to heat. All the old pains have been playing up – my shoulders are ruined from lifting what I shouldn't, timber, pallets, and my hands often lock. Sometimes I convinced myself I was in permanent remission. Maybe I was like one of the last, miraculous great elms in the park, unaffected by blight. Or I'd found the trick of acceptance – psychologists have told me I have a high tolerance for uncertainty, as if I didn't know. I'm sure now. There are small blisters in the webs between my fingers. There's that deep ache, the weakening heart. It's putting itself back together inside me.

You come back too, of course – who you were when we met, and what you became. None of this returns without your feet on the stairs, your taste, the pressure against my back. You re-form in the bed, eyes bright and stunned, apologising for our mess. I remember those delusive moments when we shared the same mouthful of air, the same bloodstream, almost. I remember the scent of orange blossom from the little tree you gave me, that strange courting gift. Its wild zest – the smell of woken groves, of cologne given to visitors, and funeral parlours.

I have two names, you told me the first night, *one given at birth, one by the government.*

I asked, *which name shall I call you?*

Soon remembering, even thinking, will be difficult.

People say timing is everything, and it's true. You arrived just as that brilliant, ill star was annunciating. I imagine you as a messenger. You were the last one here before I closed the door of Burntcoat, before we all shut our doors.

o

When I was eight, my mother died and Naomi arrived. My father still lived with us then; we had a house at the edge of town, on one of the steep streets that lead up to the beacon, from which the interior mountains can be seen. It was a few days before Christmas. The summits were snow-capped, and the air was cold and paper-thin. We were shopping for gifts and my father had brought the car – the doll's house I wanted was very large, too big to carry, so I was sure it would be bought. My mother had been complaining all day of a headache. Every shop we went into made her wince.

These lights are so bright.

She kept dragging her feet and sitting down, rubbing her forehead. We'd been to the old civic library, and, unusually for her, she'd borrowed no books. My father was annoyed.

Why did you come out with a migraine? Do you want to go home?

On the walk back to the car, she stumbled. My father was walking a little ahead, to start the car and turn on the heating; he did not see. She lost her balance and fell to the pavement, kneeling for a moment in the slush, then leaning over and sitting.

Adam, she called. *Where is Edith? Is she there?*

She sounded very calm. Her words were slow.

Adam, I can't see her.

I thought she was starting an interesting game – she could be very silly and playful. *I'm not over here, Mummy*, I said, walking round behind her. *And I'm not over here.* She held up a hand, carefully touched the air.

I can't. See.

I squatted down in front of her, stared, moved my head around. Her eyes did not follow. One iris seemed like a black planet.

Dad! I called.

My father walked back to us.

Move out of the way, he said. *What is going on, Naomi? Why are you sitting there getting filthy?*

She raised her arms and my father took hold and hauled her up. When he let go, she swayed, sagged again.

He walked her across the car park, opened the door of the Volvo and helped her onto the back seat. With every step she lost power, like a toy running out of battery. She lay quietly on the red leather, her eyes wide and empty.

Get in the front, he told me.

This was the first time I'd been allowed in the passenger seat. I clicked the metal seat belt into its lock. It was baggy, set for an adult. My father started the car and drove unhurriedly, stopping at the traffic lights. For some reason I thought we were just going home. I kept turning to look behind. My mother was breathing rapidly, her eyelids beginning to droop. She tried to talk, but the words were babyish sounds. There was a clicking sound in her gullet. I looked again and her face was in a pool of lumpy fluid.

Mum's been sick. She's being sick.

OK, thank you, Edith, my father said.

I was not scared. Nobody in the car seemed scared by what was happening.

Now turn round, and sit down.

He drove to the infirmary, pulled up to the main emergency door and put on the handbrake.

Stay here, he said to me.

I want to come in too.

No, he said.

But I want to come with Mummy.

He reached across the gearstick and smacked me on the top of the legs, an awkward, pluffing whack that stung through my skirt and tights. Then he got out of the car, walked into the hospital and came out with a porter and a wheelchair. They slid Naomi from the back seat, lifted her into the chair, and I watched her being pushed inside, her body listing over. My eyes were watering, the tears refracted everything, and for a moment there were two leaning women in two wheelchairs. I blinked and one was gone. The car smelled sour. The passenger window bloomed coldly under my palm. An ambulance pulled up next to the car, and the paramedics unloaded a stretcher.

When my father came back he did not apologise. I said nothing as he moved the car to a parking space. He steered me silently inside the building, his hand pressing between my shoulder blades.

I was given children's books by the receptionist.

You look like a clever girl, she said. *I bet you can read these all by yourself?*

I listened to her speaking to the doctors, speaking to my father, speaking into the phone. They were planning to move my mother to another hospital as quickly as possible. While my father was in the toilet I slipped over to the receptionist and asked if I could see my mother.

Oh no, poppet, you can't. She's very sick. They have to do an operation.

What's wrong with her? I asked. *Is it her headache?*

The receptionist nodded, looking pleased, as if I'd answered a school question right. *Yes, poppet. She's got a blood clot on her brain. Oh, here we are . . .*

The sound of the helicopter approaching was unmistakable – the furious blades, air thumping beside the building as it landed. Suddenly, I realised everything was serious. Helicopters were used to rescue climbers who'd fallen from the ridges; they were used to save lives. For a minute I thought we would all be going, and I was lit by excitement and fear; I'd never flown before. But almost immediately the helicopter lifted again, even louder, it seemed, its rotors whining, a blaze of deafening noise. Soon it was a faraway drone.

My father took me home, made toast and asked me to go to bed.

I need you to be a big girl, Edith.

I lay looking at the luminous stars stuck to my bedroom ceiling.

In the morning he told me my mother had been airlifted to Newcastle and a surgery performed. She would have to spend several weeks in hospital.

It was a very complicated operation. They've had to do some things that mean she won't be herself for a while. She might not even know who you are.

He was wearing the same clothes as the day before. His eyes were puffy. His whole face seemed puffy, the features gathering closely together inside it.

Yes she will know who I am, I said.

He shook his head.

She's unconscious. Christine's mum is going to look after you today.

We spent Christmas just the two of us, miserably eating mince pies. The tree was undecorated; only its smell was festive and reassuring. There was no doll's house. My father had hastily bought me a coat; the tag was still in. On Boxing Day he drove over to the hospital again. I was made a fuss of by Christine's parents, given chocolates and milk. Christine asked if my mum was going to die. I lied and told her I'd ridden in the helicopter. When my father arrived to pick me up, I heard him speaking quietly to Christine's mother as I collected my shoes and coat.

It's like Frankenstein, he said. *It's absolutely horrendous.*

Every few days he made the journey across the country. I kept asking when I could see her.

Not yet, was all he'd say. *She's not well. She doesn't remember.*

On my first visit to the rehabilitation centre, my mother was sitting at a table, drawing a picture. There was a strip of stubble in her hair containing a vast, raised caterpillar scar. One side of her face seemed pulled back and lifted. I stood in the doorway, too scared to approach.

Go on, my father said. *You wanted to come. I'll get a coffee.*

He was not looking at my mother and hadn't said hello to her.

He walked away down the corridor. My mother didn't seem to notice me. She had on pale-blue pyjamas with white snowflakes that made her look younger. A nurse entered the room behind me.

You must be Edith. Your mummy's been missing you. Come in.

She walked me to the table, pulled out a chair for me. I sat. The nurse gently placed a scarf round my mother's head, covering the curved purple welt, and tied it at the back.

There we go.

But I couldn't unsee the awful wound. The picture was childish, a tree or a figure. My mother seemed confused about the line she was making, which direction it should continue in. I took the pencil from her. She looked at me. Her expression was blank and curious, like a bird assessing an item on the ground. I finished the line, drew a nest on the branch with spotted eggs inside. Her mouth opened and closed a few times, popping wetly. With concentrated, almost physical effort, she said, *ahm, na, mee*. I looked at the nurse, who smiled.

What is she saying? I asked.

The nurse put her hands on my mother's shoulders, stopped the swaying motion that had begun to increase.

She's introducing herself. She's saying, I'm Naomi.

The haemorrhage had caused massive damage, and the procedure came with its own penalties. A precise section of bone had been sawn and removed, the pristine vacuum of the organ breached. They'd mended the tissue, clipped the vessel, and the brain's flow of blood had been redirected. Against all odds, the rupture hadn't killed her. Naomi would recover, slowly, anatomically, but something fundamental was disrupted by the process of repair – the complex library of thought, memory, emotion, personality. They saved her life; they could not save her self.

The post-surgical scan had revealed a second bulge, inoperable, too difficult to reach. There was another soft red sword hanging inside her head. They must have told her after the surgery, as soon as she was capable of understanding. She processed the information as if it were part of the instructions for her recovery – a new way to live, alongside continual possible death.

Who she was, who she no longer was, defined our lives. Years later, while on an international exchange in Japan, I tried to explain what had happened to my instructor, Shun. I was studying the cedar-burning techniques I have used ever since – and living with his family. The travel bursary had come from the Malin Centre; its director had arranged six extraordinary apprenticeships, young artists 'At Home' with makers across the world. I was in a village outside Kyoto, surrounded by the enormous, livid forest.

Shun and I had become reserved friends over the months. I ate with the family, offended them gently with my ignorance and inadequate manners, played music to his children over headphones. Shun's work was exceptional, far beyond carpentry – as well as panels for the traditional buildings he made dense, blackened sculptures that sold around the world. I was his first Western apprentice, trying to get to grips with fire pipes and resins, trying to escape the corset of fine art. Shun's English was good; he'd studied in California before inheriting his father's business. I vexed and entertained him most days. He'd been showing me how to wire-brush the scorched charcoal coat, to reveal the beautiful grain beneath, and when I told him about Naomi he paused.

This word, identity, he said, *it has just arrived here. It is singular. We cannot translate it.*

Her individual character, Shun. You know what I mean.

No.

Her nature, her Naomi-ness!

I was a young art graduate, trying to test myself and develop a practice. I was lost in this strange, quiet, dissimilar place – gaijin, a bizarre person from the outside.

Shun lifted a hand towards the forest, where the cedars stood in green-lit ranks.

She is your mother. She cannot lose her nature if she is not separate.

It had seemed, then, such a beautiful denial of concept.

o

Walking to the market this morning I felt the first flurries of panic. The stalls stand close together, rows of fruit and fish and belts, and I had to squeeze past pedestrians in the narrows. The country, and most of the world, has been vaccinated so I can share public air, interact; it's no longer an offence. I had on a common white Health Service-issued mask, and might simply have seemed to be suffering a cold. I often cover my hands, if I'm working or wheeling the truck through the city. But I was wearing silicon medical gloves that I'd taped at the wrists.

It was warm; people were sleeveless, enjoying the first proper sun. This city is small; the inhabitants know each other. The cafe owners, taxi drivers, Sam directing traffic by the castle junction, and Ginny who sells amalgamated soaps and sleeps rough in the park. The vendors are used to seeing me dressed in overalls, hauling the truck along the street, sometimes with Peltors on my ears if the noise is bad, or wearing my purple-tinted glasses. They think

I'm a shabby millionaire, half of which is true. I must have looked even more the misfit with wrapped blue hands. Or what I am: infectious, paranoid.

Rostam noticed immediately. His eyes curtseyed down and then up to my face. Perhaps I imagined his quick sift of recollection, the recoil, then compensation. Some people remember; others choose not to. Accommodation has taken us a long time.

Madam, he announced. *It's a great pleasure to see you today. I have a new shipment from Damascus. Very delicate flavour. My friends in the collective gave me a special price. I can offer it to you.*

Rostam is our street king, master of the bazaar in leather and a trilby. I remember when he took over the stall, a heavy-browed young man, possessed by theatrical humility and the confidence of desperation. He knew you too, by way of other immigrants, the community network of cousins. We don't speak of you; the past is simply in us. I'm an intermittent customer to his stall. I have no use for modified tulips or palm gardens though I like the rose leaf he imports, but he treats me as if I'm royalty, someone who spends great fortunes on his bouquets.

No, I don't need tea.

I was more reticent than usual. I tried to hide my hands, explained that I wanted the blossom – the tree should already be flowering if possible, or would flower within a week. That timescale. Not later than ten days. If he could not help I would go elsewhere, I said, though I knew he would, that he trades widely beyond the market. I explained it all too urgently, perhaps, and his face fell. He reached for my awkward plastic hands and held them, warmly through the gloves. It took some willpower not to withdraw and leave. There was clattering and shouting in the market, but a familiar sound was beginning, high- and low-pitched, rhythmic. Like electrical waves, hissing along their fetch, surging and breaking. I know better than to think others hear it too, though it seems to come from their mouths, between buildings, any sonic atom.

I understand. I will get it for you.

Rostam spoke quietly, the tradesman's bluff dispensed with.

You must promise not to go anywhere else. It is my responsibility. Yes?

Yes, thank you.

He squeezed and released my hands. The kindness moved me. I knew he would not speak overtly, that I'd be spared pity. He's a man who understands masks, what they won't admit, what they reveal by their deception. I walked away, pressing my fingers on my ears, and stood for a while under the chestnut tree by the bicycle rank, where the broad leaves absorb the city's energy, the assaulting noise. I looked towards the cafe, which is painted dark blue now and has an iron bench outside that pigeons shuffle and sit along.

I've been inside a few times – the coffee is good, affordable, free of chicory. It's been several different establishments since you owned it – a vegan deli, a sewing shop. For a while it was a ramen bar. I sometimes sat in the window holding my bowl, thinking about Shun's wife, Umeko, how she would politely correct my technique, as if I were a child. The yolks of the eggs on her exquisite dishes like the orange eyes in the centre of the cedar trunks. It used to be a tiny place, with room for only seven tables, but they've opened up the second and third floors. Even with different coats, even repurposed, the memories remain.

Which name shall I call you?
The first. Halit.

Above the window was a sign – For Sale. And by the entrance a soft warping to the air as if steam was venting from inside. I turned and walked home a different way.

o

It was January when I first went to the cafe. The name was painted on the architrave. Biraz. The place didn't seem to know what it was – there were shelves of books by the bar, plants too big for the seating area, textiles mounted on the wall, embroidered pomegranates, enamelware. There was a photograph by the till, a man in a fifties hat, crescent-eyed and gaunt, sitting with his dog on a boat. In tiny ceramic vases, stems of rosemary and lemon balm. People were drinking – coffee, wine, rakı. At one table a game of backgammon was being played. There was only one member of serving staff, a young woman who seemed overwhelmed. And behind the kitchen curtain – you.

My friends – Kendra and Bee – had heard the food was excellent and were disagreeing about what kind of cuisine it was. North African, Middle Eastern, fusion. There was no menu; a series of dishes circulated and were chosen or declined. It was a rare evening out – I'd become reclusive and overworked, Kendra had a baby.

She'd forced me away from the studio, told me to wash and tidy myself, and had left the baby with her mother-in-law, determined to eat something she hadn't cooked herself.

This is what passes for glamour, she'd said when I opened the door and she saw my flannel shirt. *At least undo that top button, love. Let's go before I start leaking.*

My hair had grown to a reasonable length, everything had calmed after the recent, wild success, and the loss of myself. My bones had sunk back into my flesh.

Do we have to do this? I'd asked.

It was cold outside. The air was stiff and had the gunpowder-and-salt smell of winter; the month already seemed dead. I'd been working in gloves and a hat in the freezing studio.

Haven't you heard there are terrible things going on? Wars, mega-bugs, Nick's mother. Live while you can.

Kendra ratched around in her bag, found a lipstick and held it out.

Here. Kahlo Red.

We'd drunk most of a bottle of wine when the first dish arrived. The waitress had disappeared. You walked from the kitchen towards our table, holding a bowl so delicately in your hand it might have been a nest. The hazelnuts had somehow been surrounded by spiced sugar; each was floating inside a glass case. You placed the bowl in the centre of the table, and then, though it was not out of position, you adjusted the knife at my place setting. There was a lithe grace to the way you moved, like a muscled, upright cat. The blue of your eyes glinted, seemed deposited, as if there was a greater mass of colour behind. I stared at you through your series of questions. Was the wine acceptable? Were we comfortable? Did anyone not like octopus?

I adore octopus, Bee said, though she hated seafood.

I don't believe in inevitability. I didn't really believe in anything, other than my work. It's not that I knew you, or didn't. I just couldn't stop looking. The astonishing speed of desire. Construction of bones. Volumes of the body. Scent. This is how it begins, with physical intuition. You were talking to my friends, casually, answering Kendra's questions, and seeing, mostly, me. Yes, this was your restaurant. Yes, you knew The Anchorman, which was owned by her husband. No, you were not French, your accent was often mistaken. I noticed Bee staring too, with less intention. She was married, as good as. I was the solitary one, had exited a series of relationships I couldn't ignite or sustain, had declared, fatally at thirty-two, that I could only commit to art. You smiled, at our group, at me, then excused yourself and returned to the kitchen. The curtain swung closed.

Finally the blood's started moving south!

I turned back to the table and Kendra was smirking at me.

I drank too much, enough to get free of myself, flirted with the men playing backgammon. You smiled every time you entered the dining area; then, because I'm no gamer, the conveyance became something else. Precognition. Promise. We were travelling through what would happen, the wet map of intimacy, the abandonment.

Was the dinner OK? you asked as I was paying. *How was everything for you this evening?*

The others had gone, purposefully, insisting I act. The

restaurant was empty, the boards and counters put away, the waitress had vanished. There was a flaw in one of your irises, silver-grey, like the broken tip of a knife.

I liked the dish with the mulberries.

The tabbouleh?

Yes.

Thank you. I'm glad you liked it.

You took the cash, gave me the receipt. I had a resin mark on the sleeve of my shirt, reddish, like a wine spot.

Bak, you said, taking hold of the cotton cuff.

You reached for a napkin, tried to blot the mark. Your hair was tied back under the chef's bandana, your dark beard was cut close, framing your mouth.

It won't come off, I said. *It's pine tar.*

You hadn't touched my skin at all, though one finger was underneath the cuff – the courtesy was exquisite. My arm fell slowly as you released it. Perhaps I still smelled of smoke and sap, though I'd been in the bath. I knew what I was. I felt myself rise, as if from the undergrowth, like a creature standing stark against the landscape.

Would you like a drink? I asked. *With me.*

The smile faded, your eyes uncreased at the corners and lost their glimmer, and the congenial host disappeared.

Now? Ah. It will take me forty minutes to finish, maybe one hour. I need to clean the kitchen and get changed. It will be very late.

I wasn't sure if you'd said no, so I stood stupidly, saying nothing, a dull feeling spreading through my chest. You seemed caught between problems, and suddenly I was aware there were rules, a finesse to exchanges that I didn't possess. My candour was a breach. You calculated something, nodded.

I can meet you. Please choose where we should go.

Near the river was a bar that served late coffee and cocktails. I found a table in the corner, played with the soft wax of the candle, wondering what fantasy I'd created and then ransacked. In the bathroom mirror I looked at myself, put water in my hair, opened a button on my shirt. On the end of its chain was the gold peacock feather, one of the few items of jewellery I owned. You arrived quicker than you'd said you would, and looked different out of the white jacket, dressed in jeans and a faded shirt. Your hair was long, to the collar. You'd put on deodorant, but there was still the smell of cooking, fryer oil and garlic. Some spell was gone, replaced not by disappointment but unpreparedness. You kissed both my cheeks. When you spoke, you seemed less fluent – nerves, perhaps. I didn't know whether to apologise for my approach. In the restaurant I'd seen and almost felt the sex, the skin's heat and sheen, and slick of viscous white. In the bar we were stripped back, had to begin as children making friends in a deliberate way, looking for something to share.

Where are you from?

I'm a mix. I moved countries. My English teacher was Scottish. I've actually been here ten years. I'm sorry – I didn't ask your name.

It's Edith.

Edith. That's nice.

You introduced yourself, formally, succinctly gave the reasons for dual citizenship, your family's expulsion during childhood. The explanation seemed rote, as if it had been given many times.

I'm called after my grandfather.

What's your other name – the Christian one?

Konstadin Konstadinov. He's the one who is officially here on the documents.

I told you I'd changed my name too. You seemed pleased and did not ask why.

What is pine tar?

It's a preservative. I use it sometimes for waterproofing wood.

Are you a carpenter?

Sort of. I make things – usually for outside. They're quite big.

I'm not really a chef. I studied chemistry.

We talked about the city, music, past lives, in which the first stories of hardship and unbelonging were revealed. Somehow, though we lived within a mile of each other, we had never met. The drinks crashed inside the barman's tumbler; they were strong, clarifying. The bottles on the shelf were unrecognisable, turquoise, red, like an apothecary's. We were the only ones there, and our solitude seemed important. The world was suspended. When the bar shut we walked along the icing river, our breath like smoke.

The date was oddly innocent. It was not until we said goodbye on the towpath and kissed that the truth of what I'd imagined was exposed. Your mouth was soft inside the sharp beard, tasted of anise. The moist flare of your tongue was an accelerant. I found myself pulling your hips close. You pressed me against the cold, iron-belted wall and continued as two drunks walked past, our state more stupid than theirs. It was as if the air had become suddenly toxic. When we pulled apart it felt like drowning. We could only breathe with our mouths held together.

o

Burntcoat stands at the edge of the old industrial part of the city, where the riverbank links workers' cottages, trade buildings and docks. Friends with houses in the Victorian wards thought I was mad to want to live here, until I explained how much space I needed. The building's records are incomplete so I don't know what its primary purpose was. Storage, auction, an exchange for cattle and cargo brought upstream from the estuary, or perhaps it was used to mend masts. It was half-ruined when I bought it, full of pigeon shit, cans and condoms. Almost two centuries of disrepair and illicit use had left it scarred, historically unlisted and cheap. The name is inexplicable in the deeds – some eponymous merchant's, an incendiary event. I admit, the name made me want the building, as well as the proportions. Such things shouldn't be meaningful, but they are. Even renovated, Burntcoat is ugly by most standards, a utilitarian warehouse, but it stands beside the river's lambency – a hag in a bright mirror. Sometimes people pause on the road outside, trying to read the writing on the bricks.

This section of river is slow and opaque, with acidic willows above the metal sidings, chained entry points and steps that disappear down into the water. Graffiti on the bridges. Skeins of debris and oil on the surface. The old wooden boathouses have been demolished or have buckled with rot, the mills converted into chic flats now.

After art school and the collective, my early luck, I thought about moving back to the uplands, but it seemed nostalgic, the territory of the past. Naomi's world; after her illness she'd abandoned herself in the wild. Instead, I settled at the region's edge, where the landscape opens into sky, and there are people, trains to the capital, a different kind of absentia. I've come to love the middle-place, the derricks and drowned roots, hidden culverts, algae-stained boats and the river's chandlery.

In the year of Naomi's rehabilitation, my parents' relationship deteriorated rapidly. How happy they'd been before, what cracks there might have been, I can't say. My father ran the local playhouse, Naomi was an author; they were prominent, artistic figures in the town. No doubt there were jealousies, scales of success – I've seen it frequently since, most dangerously when the women ascend. And also when they fall.

No one believed she would ever write again. When she was moved back to the beaconside house she still couldn't function, mixing up words, breaking things, wetting herself. There were house fires, overflowing baths, fish tucked into sock drawers. It was like absurd theatre.

Pass me that table I want to put it on. It looks onions outside.

Funny, I thought, and my laughter seemed to make Naomi feel better. My father grew impatient.

You're not helping, Edith. She isn't joking.

For him there was shame. Naomi had no sense of embarrassment, no longer cared about her appearance. Once she'd worn stylish hats, an embroidered Russian coat with a collar of feathers. She'd had an agent. Now she didn't wash properly and picked her lips, made strange lowing noises if she was anxious.

She was visited by a speech therapist each week.

Click, cluck, clock. Sing, wrong, thing.

Give me a silly sentence and a sensible sentence, Naomi.

Put your tongue out. Wide mouth. Kiss shape.

For a while we were reading at the same level, and we would sit together, sharing my comics and adventure stories. She was like a big, disabled sister. I tried to help, learnt how to make tea, brushed my own hair, put the laundry on. Little things she'd done that I knew would annoy my father I claimed as my mistake or cleaned up. The egg cracked open on top of the television.

I could feel his resentment mounting. There were other frustrations. Where her emotions had been, imperviousness now existed. She had no recollection of ever loving him. I could hear arguments in other rooms.

You're not the woman I knew, Naomi, not my wife. What do you expect me to do?

During the worst, he would shout and slam doors while she stared blankly. In the end I think he believed she was doing it on purpose, that she'd decided to vanish from her old life. He would stand in front of her, holding one of her books.

This, this is who you are.

He tried to take me with him when he left, bundling me into my Christmas coat and pushing me towards the front door. I struggled out of his grasp and ran back to Naomi and stood behind her.

Come here, Edith, now.

Naomi picked up a fire poker. She raised her arm. She was humming quietly, the notes minimal and off-key, like a church song. I was electrified and filled with horror. She'd given no sign of being roused by any kind of strong feeling since before the operation.

You are fucking beyond me. Enough. Edith, come here, please.

I didn't understand the raised edge to his voice, the desperation. I shut my eyes and gripped the back of Naomi's skirt. Some part of me knew I was making a bad choice, selecting someone who did not exist any more, and chaos.

Fine. I'll file for custody.

The door shut.

To check my mother would be able to cope with me, we were allocated a social worker. Her name was Cheryl Bone. Her hair was crimped and dry and she wore thick, buckled sandals. I hated her the moment she walked in. She followed us round the house asking questions, observing Naomi cook, noting how she dealt with me. She spoke in a grandmotherly falsetto.

Do you think it's appropriate to let Edith up into the loft by herself? Do you think her painting on the walls is appropriate? Are Edith's shoes appropriate for wet weather? I'm not here to criticise, she said, I'm here to make sure we stay afloat. Imagine I'm a safe ship.

This interference was met with Naomi's remedial logic, my bellicose opposition, our swiftly developing protectorate.

But paper is expensive and a waste, Cheryl. She's made a gallery.

If you tell Mummy you're a ship it's confusing because she'll think you are a ship.

Naomi was improving; released from my father's expectations her progression was noticeable. Perhaps she understood the stakes were higher now. An unburnt piece of toast, a tin of ravioli heated in a pan, the gas flame turned off afterwards. Remembering that I had to go to school, that Monday was the start of the week. She asked for help completing benefit forms. She spoke to a solicitor, the bank manager. I might have been in danger, but it couldn't be proved. The safety assessment showed me capable of a range of activities well above my age. The court proceedings ended, and I was allowed to stay with my mother.

Some nights I crept into bed with her while she was sleeping. Her skin, and her smell, hadn't changed.

The truth is, life was harder. I had more responsibility and no guidance. School was difficult after the free, autodidactic state of home. The teachers were patronising, the lessons useless. After the first set of tests I was marked as educationally substandard. Naomi was called in and shown the paper. I hadn't read the questions, or if I had I'd ignored them. Instead, the column of multiple-choice circles was pencilled in to create a man wearing big boots.

I think Edith is learning other things, she told the headmaster. *Can you test those?*

I was made to take the exam again, and passed. Naomi retook her driving test and passed. My father stopped paying maintenance. I hadn't seen him for almost a year.

The divorce went through. Naomi said one day,

I don't like this house. It's wrong. It's . . .

She searched for a word, couldn't find it. She found a cheap cottage on the upland moors, at the dead end of a narrow road flanked by rowan and gorse. Truss Gap. A place half done, half said. It was like a dwelling from a storybook, ingathered and overgrown, primed for disaster. Inside, the rooms smelled of clay and stone, soot and horsehair. The cottage had no mains electricity, but there was an old generator and a waterwheel, which often clogged with fallen branches and earth washed down the fellside. The garden contained two ancient apple trees and its flowers had been seeded by wild spores. A tall deer gate opened onto wilderness, marsh, ghylls, the end of the world. Close by, where the mountain rose, peat-black waterfalls hammered into bottomless pools. During winter the torrents were locked in frozen pillars, and in summer I swam all day, my skin chilled and lunar-white.

The move was good for Naomi. She didn't have to see people much, dress conventionally or struggle to behave. She planted vegetables and kept quail in a hutch, their tiny eggs like an ink-stained sky. But there was a deeper defrayal – a kind of accord, I think – in accepting jeopardy. The river swollen and roaring after heavy rain, the great, bullying wind at the head of the valley. She might be taken at any time; she knew it and was offering herself.

Often I'm asked, what was my childhood like? Was it instrumental? I was measured against the mountains, everything was. I loved Truss Gap, and the vastness of what surrounded us. Underneath, the tow of the place was strong, frightening. Its immense, shifting plates, its scale of giants and Dire wolves. We slept to the sound of moving water and I would dream of the house being washed away, of being in a stone boat, swept into a dark, underground lake, that other place.

Children adapt, fill the gaps. I was so little, and so able. I didn't miss my friends. If I fell climbing trees and Naomi seemed baffled by my noise, by the red substance trickling from the gash, I would remind her to fetch a plaster. When girls from the village school came over to the cottage to play, Naomi performed the part of a mother, copying what she saw the others doing and saying.

Would you like milk and biscuits, sweethearts?

Then forgetting to bring them.

My schoolmates were curious; their parents no doubt speculated about us. We'd arrived like refugees and had the look of mendicants.

Is your mum an actress?

Why does she talk like that?

Is she handicapped?

The village children were the sons and daughters of farmers; they were practical, sceptical. Naomi didn't walk with calipers; she hadn't lost an arm.

She teaches, I told them. And to those I could trust, Kendra first, a half-truth. *She's got brain damage from an accident.*

Naomi didn't return to work in any sustained way. She published one short novel in the following years, which was regarded as bizarre, lesser, as outsider art. It was written on brown baking paper, typed up by a local woman because Naomi could not operate the Olivetti she'd previously used – the positions of the letters confused her, and the sound of the keys was aggressive. Without any sense of triumph or retreat, she set up a writing workshop and set aside her own craft.

What should I compare those years with? A civil life? It was ordinary; it was ours. Naomi and I grew round each other like vines that need mutual support to be upright. She signed official documents, the chequebooks. She held the licences. I drove us home on the concrete road when we'd been shopping, no higher than second gear. I wrote the number of bottles on the milkman's list, learnt how to choke the generator to restart it. When we got important news, of a bereavement, or my gold gymnastics certificate, I would draw portraits with Naomi's face in the appropriate expression, sad or happy, shocked. She would nod and try to remember it.

On my birthdays I received a letter from my father, who had emigrated. The stamps were beautiful, flowers and buffalo, winter motifs. When it was legally permitted, I changed my surname to Naomi's maiden name – Harkness.

o

I'd like to say to Naomi, I understand. It's taken half my life to appreciate that cold breath on the neck. Every day she must have felt it.

And I would like to talk to you, properly, not with retrospect or yearning, the space that lies between us.

I never brought you to the valley. I described it; the sheer granite slabs, the fast brackish water and luminous moss. You never took me home either. Between coordinates is where we existed. Perhaps that's true for all relationships. In the end, we want versions we can't have, rearrangements in time. We want someone wise and scarred from the other side to say how it is, and what will happen, to be re-childed. I tell myself that the reasons are practical, companionable; it's simply about having my hand held to cross a difficult stretch, the way Naomi would take mine to get across the gullies on the moor.

Jump, Edith. It isn't deep.

This morning I sat looking at my phone, scrolling the numbers. Some I haven't been able to delete. There are friends I should probably inform. I'm acting like a cat, slinking away to the roots of a quiet tree, squeezing into a hiding hole. Karolina would come immediately. She would board the train north, carrying her small bag with a nightgown, her pills, a book; she would have some matchless phrase. And Jonah, who I haven't seen for years but whose photographs are still on the wall, of me, of Burntcoat while it was being converted. Jonah would laugh.

Get out now, darling. At least you're not pissing a hundred times a day and suffering a prick like rope.

And then he'd weep like Lear. He will be the one to forge true old age; he's escaped all the black dogs, all the predictions. For that, I'm glad.

There are others in this situation; I could read the message boards and visit support groups. There are registered services, doulas to help relapsers through it – they do everything, from existentialism to excrement. Veterans like me are celebrated, not just for biological luck but for sagacity. So many became reckless once they knew they hadn't beaten it, burning through the days, experiencing everything they could. Others became reclusive, obsessed with every cough, every headache, nerve-damaged, mind-damaged. Some are still enlisted in trials. I don't share their disbelief. I've been asked about this too. How is it possible to live with fear and hope?

I have no real interest any more, not in the thing itself. Its composition. Its character. Is it alive or dead? We are not separate; I continue, it continues. I admire its cleverness, and patience, storing away fragments in my cells, confounding biologists and immunologists. I've grown tired of waiting, I've told myself I would not wait, nor try to outrun it. You wouldn't let me forget anyway. And I had work, such terrible fucking possession. Downstairs is the proof, my national obligation. There's a burden to remembering, a duty no one really wants – all those names on the government list that have taken so long to embed. Now everything is finally happening, and I keep going to the studio to look, though the stairs are tiring and I shouldn't waste my energy. I keep calling Sean, asking stupid questions about the iron pad, the bolting, as if the thing might topple onto whichever royal is doing the unveiling. It's always like this before installation.

Every time you ring me to check the charts I think they've pulled the funding or you've changed your mind again, Sean said to me yesterday. *Stop fretting. Do you want to come to the site?*
I can't.
The steps are almost in.
OK. Good.
So, it's a green light, then?
Green light.
Sean laughed.
We must be setting some kind of record for lateness.
Sagrada Família.
Well, I'm not doing this again.
Neither am I.
Obviously. You're about halfway up, by the way.
You mean a third? H.
Pedant.

Sean was a monumental mason before he went to art college. There's not much he doesn't understand about memorials, commemorating the dead, and there are almost no technical hurdles he can't overcome. I once asked him if he believed in spirit, whether it informed the way he installed pieces. We were raising the Scotch Corner Witch by the side of the motorway. It was the largest project either of us had undertaken, two years of collaboration and a doubled budget, half the capital swallowed by the foundations. Hecky, we had pet-named her. The rain was almost horizontal, stingingly cold, and we could barely see the Hi-ab. The pack road, built to get the wagon and the forklift onto the island, was disintegrating. The sunken concrete plinth had been very slow to set; it was vast and deep. She'd been over-engineered and comprehensively insured, a forty-foot structure, dangerously close to traffic. She'd been wet-cut, burnt using techniques I'd only just mastered, varnished and tarred. The blackened timbers of her skirt seemed to be bleeding evilly in the rain.

I have a feeling, about her . . .

Do you mean she is monstrous? Sean had shouted at me as the key-wood was lowered, his hood blown off, his face red and streaming. *She better had be!*

There is art, the item, or the concept. And there is the story of art, which is not its interpretation, not its meaning.

o

I was twenty-nine when I bought Burntcoat. I'd just won
the Galeworth medal, and a staggering amount of money.
The Witch had been standing at the Scotch Corner
junction for a year, her controversy also rampant. Hecky
had divided the nation. She was magnificent, unique,
a testament to the creativity of the north. She was an
eyesore, an obscenity; there were petitions to remove her.
The commission had been unprecedented and windfallen
– I'd been interviewed along with several artists, all men,
all with solo exhibitions and pieces in the Royal Academy
shows. Without a gallerist, I'd developed a practice in
artist-run spaces, and abroad, surviving on Arts Council
grants and occasional patronage. Sean had mounted big
industrial-estate art, and after Japan the Malin Centre
had paired us and continued to support me for off-site
work. He'd installed two of my sculptures in the private
park at Hadrian – native oak and hazel, burnt using an
adaptation of shou sugi ban. Their scale was unusual
for a woman, it was said, unusual even for a land-artist.
With only weeks to prepare, I was invited to apply for
one of the largest public art commissions ever conceived.
She was not dreamt, like Mendeleev's table, though she
seemed in my mind an element, absolute. Sean knew
what I wanted to do, and how to do it.

In the interview I was asked if my proposal was realistic, whether it would exceed the funding, who my influences were. My answers were brief, disengaging. González, Gentileschi, Oppenheim – her Bern fountain with its tufa and lichen, I said. I did not anticipate success, so had nothing to lose. It was a panel of four judges, three were women – one an arts officer I knew to be progressive, more of a scout, one a historian, and there was a woman I did not know, dressed in grey plaid and moleskin, who looked suited to hand-start the propeller of a biplane. I don't know what tipped the balance. My age and sex. My incongruity. Perhaps it was because I knew the road the piece would be gatekeeper of, the desolation of the summit, its storms. Hecky herself; she seemed undeniable.

These model sketches, the male judge said, *are really compelling, but, how shall I put it, very strong meat. Is she – squatting?*

No. She's unfurling. The junction island is covered in gorse and gorse flowers every month of the year. It'll look like she's rising from the flames.

So she's being punished? Doesn't that send a bad message?

She's rising, I repeated. *She's not supposed to be mystical.*
The man scowled.

OK. But this Asian process you use. Isn't the wood going to rot, in a maritime climate?

Not for half a millennium.

I watched his eyebrows ride high on his forehead. It was more or less the truth.

They've found prehistoric spears here with burnt tips, I explained. *They're more resilient. So it's not really a 'foreign' technique.*

I was trying, and failing, not to sound arrogant. The historian was nodding.

I just don't see how this type of thing can be achieved. It's enormous. It would horribly overrun. And the attention would be . . . well, very difficult to manage. We've already had the bishop's cursing stone to contend with.

There was a snort from the woman in plaid. She leant forward, peering through her winged designer glasses.

If I may, William. Ms Harkness. How would you feel about the council owning the drawings and models? I think that might provide some fiscal surety. Would that be fair?

It's fine by me, I said.

There was no way of knowing what would come, what I was signing away. I had no idea that this was Lady Ingrid McKenzie, whose father had built a munitions fortune and whose grandfather had deposed a prime minister. She donated to national galleries. She owned the land surrounding the site.

There we are. And I for one would like to hear more about your techniques, native or otherwise.

o

Learning the practice had been revolutionary, and Japan was astonishing. Shun had met me in the airport with instructions to stay at the Meeting Point – I would never have found my way out. I was jet-lagged and disorientated; the signage was impossible, my rucksack was huge and heavy and I lumbered through the futuristic arrivals hall. On the bullet train, the towns flew past. I'd been told about punctuality, and the timing was exact. Another train, a bus, nature was repeated in the architecture. After a formal introduction, Shun spent the journey talking about his years in California, where he'd studied business and economics, and where he'd tried pot and Birkenstocks. As we passed through the landscape he pointed to the red flying gateways. They were everywhere.

The residency was designed as immersive, life and craft together. I stayed in a tiny house a short walk away from Shun's family and his workshop. The grandfather house. It was immaculate and compact, the rooms no bigger than four mats, the timbers original, black and alligatored. The house was raised above the ground and seemed to hover in the electric-green forest.

For the first few weeks Shun would walk over to collect me, kind and insistently paternal. Umeko would make our breakfast, and their children, Ayumi and Eiji, would stare, giggle when I sipped silently from my bowl, and be chastised by their parents. Then Shun and I would cycle to his workshop.

As his father and grandfather had, Shun worked with traditional pipe kilns, a variety of brushing methods and oils, but he also used industrial flamethrowers, state-of-the-art equipment – I was expected to become proficient with both. He worked only with cedar, the wood most receptive to deep burning, and was amused by my immediate questions, my keenness to experiment. He knew by looking at the cut trunk and quality of bark which wood was best. I was given a heat-repellent jacket, though Shun did not wear one. He squatted close to the kilns, kept a careful distance from the blue tongue of the torches. There was incredible skill to it – collapsing the cell walls to strengthen the wood, preserving its integrity while enhancing its beauty. Too much heat and the piece was ruined, too little and the wood wasn't sealed, could not achieve the finish. Shun called this experience.

The wood is experiencing fire now. It will be improved.

A slight, whimsical smile, as if I was being instructed in life philosophy too. Sometimes he was half playing a part. He'd lived in America, seen the films; he understood what was expected of a master. I would tease him gently.

Shun, shouldn't you wear an eyepatch, like Chihuly?

Shun, shouldn't you grow your beard longer?

When I asked if I could play music in the workshop he had a long list of requests from the life before his restoration to the land of ancestors.

I've since taught others shou sugi ban. It's counter-intuitive – damaging wood to protect it. Trust comes only after patience; to begin with I had neither. Shun's grandfather had made the panels of the local temples. Shun was respected across Japan. I watched him extinguish with water in a way that looked half holy, half menial; he knew exactly how to control the blurting flames, how to time the fire's afterburn. In a matter of hours he would achieve fossilisation, that which would take river mud or peat a thousand years.

But it was in the brushing stage that his artistry showed. He would turn back his sleeve, never soil it. The motions were beautiful. Under the charred coat, the true grain was revealed, in dark vectors and knots, patterns so suggestive they became stories. Once the surface was sealed and finished, Shun would apply one single drop of water, a perfect sitting bead. Then he would step away, as if encouraging my private moment of consideration.

Do not force the fire. Respond to it.
Do not drown the wood. Moderate rain, as the English say.
The brush should travel only natural roads.

At the end of each day we would cycle back to the house and eat dinner. Aromatic curries and soft rich eggs, red-bean cakes enclosed in leaves cut from Umeko's lovely garden. She spoke almost no English so Shun translated.

Umeko asks if you are warm at night?

Yes, very comfortable.

Would you like to use the telephone to call England?

No, thank you – my mother never answers the phone. I'll write to her.

I liked being lost. I liked the routines, times when solitude was expected, bathing, reading, the lighting of lamps. I was immersed but couldn't access something innate, something intangible. Umeko could see. Once, she smiled at me and held up a hand, its fingers splayed. She wove the first finger of her other hand between them – an imaginary weft thread. Ayumi was nine and fascinated by my clothes, the dyed T-shirts and silver jeans, my blue fringe.

My daughter says you are a peacock with no tail, Shun told me.

After dinner I would help clear and wash, then play with the children, running after them, meowing and cawing. I would walk back to the grandfather house in the arboreal dusk, the leaves above luminescing and murmuring like the low voice of a woman. The morning sun behind the forest was golden and open, the mouth of a fish.

At weekends I sometimes travelled to the cities, where architecture changed almost overnight, modernist buildings regenerating beside paper houses and narrow alleys, and I made trips out to the islands, to the galleries and museums.

Be ready to accept both states together, Shun said. *They are not opposites. You'll see!*

He advised me to go to certain gardens, designed for retreat, for rain or serenity. I carried communication cards, held them up like a mute. I sat at the back of empty buses, pressed into commuter trains where the sweat of strangers slicked my arm. The country was fast and still, ancient – and advanced beyond anything I'd known. It folds outward and inwards in my memory. Inversions and parallels, upper and lower worlds. The mountains and trees were symbols, their own imperial shrines. The temples were perfectly maintained, even the oldest, with mist arranged at their wings. Everywhere, the red arches, the sacred borders, as if at any moment I could pass through to some unreachable place.

And from silent spaces to streets so frenetic; no one looked me in the eye or smiled, no one held doors, yet the politeness was faultless, so inherent it could not be called etiquette. I repeated phrases, *sorry, my fault, excuse me,* and faces lit up. In eating rooms I had to point at the menu and choose, or shrug and say, *you decide*. Men offered me drinks. The women were curious, stunning. Everything I'd read and anticipated seemed like a fetish.

I went to Storm House. Adachi. Haguro. When I entered Teshima, a domed installation Shun had insisted I visit, I understood some form of perfection had been achieved. The space was total, its own mind. Through the oculi, sky itself was art, and light travelled in moons across the wall. Groundwater rose through a million pressure holes in the floor, and droplets shifted towards others, joining, trickling, playing with their own constant difference. It was chaos and peace. Nothing had prepared me for the emotion I felt there, the acceptance, finding myself in tears and becoming part of the flood.

Then, back to the forest, its radiant enclosure, and back to the workshop where I learnt to destroy to create. I began to think I might stay beyond the residency.

One morning, as I was using a wire brush on the burnt timber, I felt a presence behind me. Shun had taken to leaving me alone. We'd dispensed with the many rituals, and once I was adept he considered it impolite to observe my work and would wait until everything was complete before discussing it. I turned. Umeko was there with

Shun – she did not usually come to the workshop. I kept brushing. The charcoal skin was soft and unset.

Shun waited until I had cleaned the swarf. He looked stiff with concentration and was wearing a different coat, formal, fastened to the neck, though it was July and very humid. He came towards me, stopped two arm-lengths away and asked for my forgiveness. I've done something wrong, I thought, offended. He lowered his head, then looked at me and told me that my mother had died. The news had only just been relayed to him. Umeko walked forward and stood beside me. Without touching me, she moved me to the bench to sit.

Most of my life I'd been expecting it. I'd grown out of the panic of the first years, running into her room, checking for breath, searching for her figure on the moors; I'd found ways of holding the possibilities internally. At some moment, every day of my life, I had considered the chance. Not yet that morning, or, if I had, the thought had passed unnoted, a bird's swift reflection crossing the river. I told Shun.

I haven't thought about it today.

He misunderstood, assumed some kind of failed conveyance.

It is a shock. A terrible accident.

I thought about it yesterday. When I woke up.

It was in the evening.
No.

He apologised again, was braced for discomfort, possible failures of language and failure of care towards the young woman so far away from home. But it was not words or culture that caused the confusion. Naomi had died in a car accident. She had not been the driver. Shun had to repeat it several times, and each time it was worse for both of us.

On the plane home I kept thinking, no, it's not right, the autopsy will show the truth, another rupture, she must have fitted in the seat while the friend was driving, instigating the crash. I was too angry to cry. The idea that Naomi's fate had not been delivered properly was impossible to accept. The universe had corrupted their deal.

England looked as vibrant as Japan as the plane flew over. On the ground it seemed ugly, dirty and in disarray. People were loud and careless. The bins overflowed and the transport system was torpid. The director of the Malin had been contacted by the police, and she'd been the one who had spoken to Shun. She'd arranged the new travel tickets, though Shun had insisted on paying the fare himself, stewarding me discreetly through the procedure of getting home, reversing our first journey, expecting me at any moment to shatter. At the airport, unusually overcome, he had bowed and walked away. I slept on the slow train north, hot summer air buffeting through the top window, my rucksack propped on the seat next to me like a shield. In its front pocket were two blue paper birds the children had made for me.

I took the key from the nook in the stonework. The cottage smelled of Naomi's clothes, her skin and pheromones. A week-old cup of tea was next to the sink, half-finished, its meniscus white and thick. I lay on her bed, wakeful, my body clock set to another zone, and imagined Ayumi and Eiji running in her overgrown garden, out onto the moorland and up to the waterfalls. I wanted to walk back into Teshima, take off my shoes, stand mindlessly and find no significance in any risen tear.

o

You stopped at the staircase and looked up, confused, the first time you came home with me. We'd walked again along the river in the cold graphite hours after midnight. What would happen was unspoken. Burntcoat was notorious and formidable, not the kind of place where anyone would reside.

Do you live in a han?

You quietly read a few of the words painted by Jonah on the brickwork.

They have escaped their mud turrets and flown upwards.

They have moulted and hardened, blue-black and golden,
treasures from the Pharaoh's tomb.

The handwriting looked faint, spectral. I took you inside
via the fire escape, and you didn't see the studio.

As we went up the narrow iron steps, you touched my
back, then my hip, my calf. You'd taken off your glove
and your hand was the only point of warmth in the eye of
winter. The bag you were carrying scraped gently on the
wall like stiff feathers. The streetlight barely reached the
industrial border of the city and the sky was seeded with
stars. If I'd turned, I would have seen an empty space filled
with shadows instead of your face.

There's blindness to new lovers. They exist in the rare
atmosphere of their own colony, trusting by sense and feel,
creatures consuming each other, building shelters with
their hopes. Other worlds cease. I know I felt something
as it began, an understanding, foreboding, ordinance, even.
Love is never the oldest story. It grows in the rich darkness.

There was no exact event. Everything bleeds together, can't
be separated. I remember breathlessness, elation climbing
through my body, charging all the nerves, unbearable
restraint. The series of breaches, exquisite touches – the
hollow below your ear, your mouth preparing me, your
hands holding my head as the smooth tip pushed past my

lips, sliding to the back of my tongue, along its live muscle. The second, third attempts, until we worked together like skinned machinery. On our sides, your forehead on my breastplate, the nipple grooming your face. My body pinned, your fingers reaching under, slick, coated.

It was impossible not to look. Your bones were prominent at the edge of the pelvis, your upper spine. Scars, along the line of your chest, the midsection, the groin, in white resolute folds.

What happened here?

Appendix.

And here?

My lung collapsed. They made a mess. Sorry.

Don't hide them. Lift your arm.

We were reckless, unprotected. I gripped you towards the end, desperate for depth, the latch. You began coming and reared back, only just in time, spilling on my belly, my shoulder.

After, you washed, and we ate food you prepared, falling on it like predators before sleeping. The white product dried on my skin, crisp and tight. You would call to me in the bath.

Do you like garlic? How much salt shall I put? I can take out the covers inside the onion – what are they called?

Membranes?

Yes. If you don't like them.

It's fine – I like onions.

Emine, my mother, she loves them but they give her too much acid.

Oh. My mother once ate an onion like an apple.

What! Why?

I began to tell you about Naomi.

I knew almost nothing about where you came from, the conflict and divided identity. There were deep, kind lines at the sides of your eyes, a crease of frustration in the centre of your brow – the chef's cut, you said. In your first language you were considered funny, a wit, speaking rapidly like a sports commentator; in English the humour was gentle, delivered. Who can say what a good match is. Through small exchanges, we built a foundation – the world is fundamental, varied, but its struggles are repetitive and similar. We both had grandfathers who had mined. Yours had been killed in a collapse along with two hundred men; mine had been photographed before the closures, walking up the return, his face filthy and fatigued as it hit the daylight, already emphysemic. When I showed you the photo, you said,

I feel like that. This winter has been so hard, not enough sun.

You pulled me to you.

What is this perfume? It's like a drug. I can't stop going there.

Your mouth against my collarbone, lips brushing my neck as softly as you could, torturing to gain permission. You pulled up my shirt. There's a crescent scar on my lower abdomen, with a rucked hole where the suture missed; you inserted a thumb, didn't comment, but asked,

What was your worst pain?

I don't know. What was yours?

Kidney stone – I take too much salt. I wanted to die. I lay on the floor of the taxi on the way to the hospital. I'm glad you can't remember.

I do remember. It was when they removed a drain from my stomach. I'd had emergency surgery. It felt like a knife sliding out – a blunt one.

Blunt?

Not sharp.

Ah, blind, we say the knife is blind. Would you like me to sharpen yours?

The next night you brought a whetstone from the restaurant. You dripped water from a hand, bent over the counter and worked the blades at an exact degree, replacing them in the drawer one by one, lethal silvered weapons I was too afraid to use.

When I was surer, I invited you into the studio.

Would you like to see what I'm working on?

Of course. Shall we go tomorrow?

I opened the door to the interior stairs – you'd stayed in

Burntcoat only a few times and were confused, imagining the space below to be abandoned. You were very serious entering, as if walking into a hallowed building. It was as cold as a crypt. I handed you a scarf from my winter work pile. I tried to explain a little; talked about the metalworker who'd taught Picasso to weld, and Brâncuşi, microbial decay. There is no good way to present what is, I know now, uncommon, almost alien. A piece was under construction in the workspace – based on the fable of the wolf and the crane, commissioned by a wealthy medical trust. The structure looked grotesque, chunks riven apart, almost like an autopsy. There were black timbers propped against the walls. I saw it through your eyes, suddenly, the occult craft room.

This is . . .

Aesop's Conundrum.

The wolf was lying submissively on its back, shingles of grey elder bark for fur, its mouth wide open – the long beak of the crane would be inserted down its throat.

Do you know the story? I asked.

Yes. But I feel like I am intruding.

I invited you. I don't mind people coming in.

No, I mean these two. It looks like this should be a private matter.

I laughed.

It is quite erotic, I suppose. There's a real bone in there. Once they're fixed together it won't be seen.

You went over to the cooker where I boiled resins, and I sat on the bench and watched.

We use the word microbe for germs, all germs. Why won't anyone see the bone?

I was used to different questions – personal or financial. I was used to walling off my identity like a dangerous cyst, being told that I was too intense, uncanny in capability; the work was too momentous for a normal partner. But you seemed comfortable around the materials, around me. Even with the brazed, formal signature on the sculpture's plinth.

It's about trust, I said. *The wolf could eat the bird. But the wolf can't eat until the bone comes unstuck. What if it's a trick? What if there's no bone? The crane won't know until its head is inside, past the teeth.*

You were still smiling.

We have to trust? Help each other. Find a cure. Is it OK to look?

Yes.

You peered into the wolf's hollow gape.

It's beautiful, like glass.

It's a fossil. It belonged to an archaeopteryx – a prehistoric bird.

She made the problem even better!

You laughed then and held out your palms. Often you talked with your body, gestures, pauses, a way of holding and releasing your pose that was cultural. I could see you thinking, quickly translating, then very casually you quoted lines of a poem.

I'm dying, my God. This is happening too.
Every death is an early death, my God.
Yet, the life you are taking wasn't too bad.
Keep the change.

You seemed comfortable, alike even, but you didn't touch me inside the studio, not then, or ever.

Upstairs I had other names, in your language, begging, sworn before climax. The stove in the bedroom kept us warm. We sat or lay, you unwinding from work, taking off layer after layer, and our forms melted together in the red underworld light. We slept as the flames settled and died, tucked together like pigeons in a loft, the sleet creeping over the roof, the country waiting. February, with its bare, larval branches. March. Other nations were closing borders, quarantining.

You brought the orange tree from the market, carried it rustling up the stairs, and we put it on the small iron balcony over the river. It was blossoming wildly. The scent was heady, urgent; it released something in us. Bodies in the rubble of a huge earthquake when you were fifteen had a similar smell, you told me. Briefly, a kind of sweet, organic rot. Then they became putrid, no one could go out;

your father had insisted you stay home.

But I went. I wanted to know what it was like. I'm sorry to say it. After a week it was so strong, awful. You could tell which buildings had people under. Stupid boy.

You looked pained, so undefended. I took your hand.

I kept the scan of Naomi's brain, the one before surgery. The haemorrhage is like a rose. It's completely horrible and beautiful too. Sometimes I look at it.

Secrets too intimate to pass without marking us, inviting trespass.

Canım.

You took me by the shoulders and brought me against you, found warm skin on my back, the soft interior of my mouth, the fastening of my jeans – extraordinary wetness you realised was blood when you undressed me.

I didn't stop you. I didn't care. Nothing can prevent desire in its first stages. Your arousal was like a drug. You put me on the floor. There was red smeared on my thighs. You kept slipping out, were agonised by the slickness of the movement, the adolescent slapping, pleasure filled with bad knowledge. The cold wind kept flushing through the open window as if trying to rouse us. Insistent, seductive perfume drifting on it. You came, saying you were going to, asking to stay inside. I raised my hips as you drove in. There was slight shame afterwards: you'd been taught doctrines. The blood smelled of fresh iron, there were small clots in the hair on your thighs. We went to wash, dried each other, a little lost by the direction we had gone, into a new room of the relationship.

That wasn't totally safe?

Maybe not. I'll go to the pharmacy.

I'm sorry. Oh God. I loved it.

Me too.

I was dripping on the floor.

You don't need to apologise, Halit.

I'm trying not to.

You watched me insert a tampon, though I'd turned and was being discreet. Another taboo broken. You sat on the corner of the bath, pulled me backwards into your lap.

Can I feel?

Inside?

Yes.

You circled your fingers, pressed one gently into me until you felt the cotton end. You slid it back out, kept stroking.

Is this right? you whispered. *I want to make you.*

I moved your hand a fraction. My head fell back on your shoulder. Your prick swelled; you pulled it away, sloped it up my back, an incidental thing. You used the tips of two fingers.

Like this?

Yes.

My nerves were already alive from the sex, the cramps. It took only moments.

○

On Saturdays I met you after closing, when the bars were already emptying. Sunday was your day off; by then you were exhausted, full of frustration that easily became lust. Afterwards you would sleep as if dead, motionless, on into the bright sunlight. Or you arrived at the apartment in the early hours, having cleaned and locked the restaurant, and I would hear the ringing of feet on the iron stairs. The night was interstitial; hours awake midway, as once there would have been field labour or prayer. You would bring small coffees to the bed, or open wine, and would talk until the night's energy had released.

It's snowing outside. Snow! English weather is so confusing – I thought it was spring. Yesterday I walked without my jacket.

Let me get up and see.

That is what I want to see – your pale ass like the moon.

It's not that white.

Yes. I'll take you somewhere hot in the summer.

Where?

Akyaka. It has a beautiful river, so cold it can give you a heart attack if you jump in.

Cold? No, I know cold water.

In the morning I would get up, go downstairs half-dressed to sit in the studio, then return to bed as if I'd never left. You'd stir, roll stiffly towards me.

Günaydın.

Hello again.

Once, as I was coming back up, I found you awake and working shirtless in the kitchen. There was orange blossom on the counter. You were heating a pan on the stove.

What are you making?

You leant and kissed my cheek.

I had a dream that I went to my grandmother's house in Bulgaria. She was very traditional and always gave visitors kolonya. I could smell it so perfectly in the dream.

You were turning the oil slowly in the pan, melting the flowers down.

What else does it need, Mr Chemist?

Alcohol. Tobacco.

I have vodka.

Sure.

I poured you a shot and drank one.

Really! I don't like vodka. OK, give it here. Hassiktir! Actually that's quite good – I do like vodka.

The perfume when it cooled was floral, refreshing, slightly antiseptic. You left it to sit and then tipped it into a small, clean spice jar.

I'm impressed. What other skills have you got?

OK. Well, I should tell you that before I came here I was in the military.
Really?
That wasn't my choice.

You put the scent on my hands and wrists.
Where do you wear your perfume?
Here.
You thumbed the liquid onto my neck, blew gently on it.
If I know you are coming, here.
Oh, to invite me.
You lifted up the long jumper I was wearing.
To do this?
You knelt down.

Adult games. We tried other experiments – which height worked best when you were behind, if I wore shoes with a heel, bent forward and held the rail of the bed. One item worn highlighting nakedness. I tightened my stance, tipped my pelvis and you forgot any mutual instinct, forgot how a woman is made. You lay on your back and I gently ran my tongue along the front and then underneath your erection, bringing the end into my mouth, before swapping again.
Which side is better? This side . . . or this side . . .
Oh God. I don't know.
Which one?

Both.

Choose.

This . . . Front. When you do that.

I lifted away. I knelt across your chest and began to touch myself. You leaned forward to see, to help, then watched the technique as if watching a stranger.

Show me how with you, I asked.

No! Come on. I can't do that?

Imagine I'm not here. Like you're in the shower.

You refused, smiling and scowling, so I started again with my mouth, and breathed.

Show me, Halit.

I knew – to call you by your name meant you would give in. You took over, held it out from your body as if separating a piece from the rest, and swiftly, soundlessly, made a white web across your stomach.

A string was broken, another spun of trust – the psychology of intimacy. You saw me looking at the tip, the dark lilac belt.

Shall I tell you about when I was cut? I was six.

You described the circumcision, a few days after your birthday. You and another boy, dressed in blue-and-white costume, were lifted onto horses and led down the street by the men in your family. The horse you rode was big, ill-tempered, it kept sidestepping, grinding the bit. You knew what was coming, everyone did, such things were not private. The other boy was braver; he let go of the reins and held the animal's mane, showing off.

I didn't know the doctor. He was probably doing fifty that day, all over Istanbul. My grandfather held me down, crossed my arms.

My head was resting on your arm and I was lying against your chest. Your body was rigid, the biceps jumped as your hands lifted, conducted the trauma in the air. There was an injection; in that way you were lucky. But you screamed for them to stop, fought as hard as you could.

I hated them all. I hated God. The other boy had to watch what was happening, so I think in the end it was worse for him.

Afterwards, bulky wadded tissues taped to the top of your legs, and a ceremony, at which you were praised, told you were a man, and money was pinned on your jacket. You had kicked so hard you'd split your grandfather's chin – *küçük boğa, little bull* – it became your nickname, the family joke.

I didn't know what to say, but you kept talking.

I went to mosque in the afternoons, and learned Arabic. I learned the call to prayer. When it echoes in the empty space it's a very strong, spiritual thing. If I heard it when I was playing football I would feel so guilty.

I turned to look – you were staring at the beams in the

ceiling, the voids. There was a glimmer in the corner of your eye.

What do you believe now?

You shook your head.

The imams gave us little sticks to point out the letters we were learning – like ice-cream sticks. I stuck two together with tape and made a cross. It didn't mean anything, I wasn't really thinking. The imam saw and took it away. He broke it, told me – never do that.

I think back on those last unrestricted months. The before. There was such freedom and faith; I've never known it again. After knowledge, after experience, comes an unmovable weight, to the body, the mind. It's like war; the effect is invasive, almost genetic. It can't be undone.

Those mornings were contradictory, fiercely sunny but still raw, with frost under the north side of buildings. We saw no one we knew; friends assumed. You went to work but the restaurant was quiet. People were worried, could feel the first sting. A few months of carefulness, masks and closures, and it would pass, I thought. I was stupid with contentment. But it was becoming the only story in the news. You checked every day, the figures coming in from the east, the different media reports and government denials. You were anxious about your family, who were nearer the main sites of the outbreak: the city of two continents, so full, so populous.

There was footage of virologists giving catastrophic estimates and nurses in the capital making video appeals.

Why is nobody doing anything? We have nowhere to treat these patients except with everyone else.

It did not seem possible joy would be disrupted, or that our bodies could break. The eye can see disaster on a screen, human silt and effluent, makeshift triages, pits, and the brain cleanly dissociates. We live temporally, deluded. Not here, not us. Of all people, I should have known better. But I thought my lot had changed. Even your cautiousness seemed like a closed window. Outside, the danger, the fear, made what was happening inside purer. The fucking of innocent gods.

Those voices, pleading for action. The zones on the map blooming red, and the red vectors between. Dreams of the rodent, the wild dog, in which it had existed, then suddenly leapt, breaking the barrier. The weeks we were together, entering the bloodstream of love, it was travelling unstoppably, like its predecessors, its sequence long and patient, transmitted by touch, fluids, breath. It had learnt to incubate, could survive outside crowds. It had perfected itself for us.

We drove to the beach, across the neck of the country; I remember the date – it was the 15th, the Ides of March.

I'd promised to show you the Scotch Witch on the way. I heard you draw breath as we approached, as she broke the horizon, her edges sharp and dark. We parked and walked the pathway to the base and you stood, speechless, at the edge of the reef of gorse. Don't let this finish, I thought.

At the coast, we walked along corrugated sand, our faces covered by scarves. The light over the sea was radiant: great vaults of shale and a bright patina to the sky. The marram grass reached over the dunes, stroked light and dark as the wind coursed through. We walked in each other's arms, in step, and from the surf a black-headed seal watched us, then disappeared. There had been a high spring tide; storm debris was everywhere. Racks of shells and dismantled carcasses, driftwood. I couldn't help myself.

Look at that. Will you help me lift it?

We hauled the large piece of salted oak back to the roadside. Its shape was bizarre, with branches emanating from its core as if the sea's fission had malformed it. The wind was bitter, scouring us with sand. We'd planned to camp on the beach but slept in the back of the van, next to the sodden oak. We acted as if we were on holiday, honeymoon, the edge of our new life. We were. The world had caught fire; not even the sea's tonic would put it out.

○

Naomi's friend – Ellen – had been pulled from the wreckage of the crash. She wanted to see me, so I went to the hospital, where she lay half-demolished, her eyes swimming up out of the medication. She whispered through her pulped jaw. They'd been on the pass, coming back from the south of the county, she said. A lorry had crossed the central reservation, hitting and flipping them. The car had rolled down the embankment, crushing in like foil. There'd been no time to think.

I can't stop hearing her. She was shouting, dee-dee, dee-dee.

Fluid ran from her eyes. I held her hand, gently. I asked if she knew about Naomi, her condition, whether anything had happened in the car. Did she say her head hurt?

No. She was fine. She never said a thing. What does it mean – dee-dee?

I think it was my baby nickname.

With the help of a neighbour, I arranged the cremation and put Naomi's belongings, and her archive, into storage. A yellow metal container for a life's worth. Her agent had long since passed away; she'd had no dealings with Saul that I knew of for more than a decade. When I called the agency I was put through to several secretaries, then the junior accountant who was overseeing the royalty stream. He had never met Naomi, was flustered over the news, and asked for a copy of the will.

The next morning, Karolina Sepehri called me back and introduced herself.

I apologise for Benjamin – he's very young, not used to people. Your mother was truly exceptional. Quite unlike any of her peers.

The accent was minimal, the pronunciation acute.

She's one of the reasons I joined the Saul Agency. What can I do to help you, Edith?

Karolina rode a train north that day, and took a parochial taxi twenty miles to the cottage. She stood under the enclosed, thundery sky, in a linen jacket, enjoying the house, the mossed roof and stacked vernacular slate. She kissed me on both cheeks when I opened the door. At the kitchen table she drank an exquisite floral tea that she'd brought in her bag and left for me on her departure. She talked briefly about the agency, her family history, the shah. She asked me very few questions, but each had the tenor of a captivated aunt. She had believed in Naomi; she seemed, immediately, to believe in me. For some reason I talked, about my childhood, the work I had done with Shun, what I hoped to become. I spoke about Naomi, our life – its ordinary and exceptional moments. She listened.

When did I know I was an artist? I've been asked so many times. As if there's annunciation, cosmic lightning. Naomi would say she knew. The summer I turned thirteen. The summer of the ship. That August she was gone most days, teaching her workshop. I accompanied her for the first few sessions, but the drive was long, the community centre was dull, attended by bored retirees and timid divorcees. I told her I preferred to stay at the cottage, that I didn't mind being alone. I said I had my own plan, and she took me at my word. We'd got rid of the social worker, Cheryl. A telephone had finally been installed. It seemed workable.

The summer was searing hot, with high blue skies, chaff drifting, a cuckoo sounding dully in the valley like a heartbeat. The marshes were drying up, and cotton grass and swarms of flies had taken over. Every morning before she left, Naomi put a basket on the table containing cheese and apples, antihistamine, little folded sanitary pads and a book about puberty – though I was still undeveloped, had a flat athletic chest – and the front-door key. I swam in the waterfalls, diving from rock pillars into the bottomless pools, holding my breath as I kicked down and down. Then I collected all the useful wood I could find, branches from the moor, planks, I took off the shed door that had been hanging on its bottom hinge. I asked Naomi to bring me more and she'd arrive home with the boot open, the back seat folded down, pallets and crates rammed in. I would hear the load clattering as the car bounced over potholes into the yard. I wanted rope, hammers and nails, old bedsheets. She didn't ask me what I was doing. I told her not to go into the bottom of the garden.

The hull was deep, copied from a picture book, made of boards and sticks. I raised the prow on rocks, so the ship was cresting waves of grass. The stern was big enough that two people could sit together tightly on crates. It took weeks of construction. I was covered with scratches and cuts, which stung as I sweated. The plague of tiny biting flies left my hairline and the folds of my elbows itching madly. I kept busy all day so I would not be waiting for the sound of the car, so I wouldn't have to think.

Halfway through the project I started telling Naomi,
  I need a wheel.
  Why?
  It's just extremely important. It has to be old.
  I pestered until she agreed to help. There were some ancient iron-rimmed cartwheels attached to the fence of a farm nearby, a kind of defunct agricultural gallery. Naomi disliked the farmer. His face was boiled red and angry, his wife tremored and took Valium, there were regular altercations about our shared gateway. We drove the car with the lights off in the eleven o'clock twilight, crept along the track and stole a cartwheel. We rolled it

to the car and lifted it in. I kept trying to hug my mother but she told me to hurry; she seemed confused about what to do and got into the passenger seat. I drove us back across the moor, thrilled, the accelerator pressed too hard for the low gear.

Go into third, Edith.

I'm not allowed.

Third!

It shouldn't have mattered how imperfect the construction was. But it did matter. I reassembled it three times, scaled it to the picture. I finally made a show of unveiling it, leading Naomi down the garden. The ship was cross-rigged, the mast and beams roped. The old white sheet drooped but looked authentic. In her inanimate way, Naomi was astonished. Her face slowly adjusted to surprise, her eyes brightened. I was her shoulder-height. The muscles below my denim cut-offs were long and lean, and she kept my hair cropped short. She stepped back and looked at me as if realising I was far beyond domestic keep.

Edith. You've made an actual ship.

Naomi was used to my inventions and experiments, but an eighteen-foot toy was something else. She walked around it, looking at the details.

Did anyone help you? she asked.

The question annoyed me, but I bit my lip.

No.

You did it. By yourself.

Then the dial clicked.

Oh, it's fantastic! she cried. *Just fantastic! Wait here.*

She ran through the garden, back inside the cottage, came out again carrying a bottle of old red wine and two mugs. She poured a measure for each of us, recorked the neck and handed it to me.

OK, she said. *Launch her. Smash this on the front. Ready?*

I threw the bottle at the side of the ship and it clonked off into the grass, unbroken.

Harder!

I hurled it and this time the glass shattered, leaving a dripping red wound on the planks and red splashes on my bare legs.

Now name her. She has to be a she, Naomi said.

OK! I name you – the Cheryl Bone.

There was a pause, and then Naomi laughed, unprompted; she understood the joke. Excitement felt like a pain in my ribs and round my heart.

Yes, she said, *yes, our safe ship, Cheryl.*

We drank the musty wine, sitting on the stern behind the stolen wheel, our arms stuck together, the terrible flies crawling up and into our hair. Naomi smelled of Nivea and oniony perspiration. Her face had recomposed itself – placid as a tarn. I felt light-headed from the alcohol. There were treatments my mother had been offered, antidepressants, hypnosis. She'd undergone psychotherapy, electric shocks. For four years, I had not heard her laugh or shout or cry.

At the end of the summer my period arrived, too heavy for the thin little pads. I hated the brown-stained pants on the washing line, the invasive ache and hormones. I squabbled with Naomi, called her names, tested out all kinds of bad feelings and tried to get a reaction.

If your stupid brain explodes I'll be fine, Mother.

She would stare at me and leave the room. I'd run outside and sit in the ship, sulking. Then, when I went back to school, she started her last story – The Reddening – which would pay off the mortgage and prove, despite everything, she could still write. In it a girl wakes one morning to find her bed covered in large, blood-eyed insects. They are in her vest and crawling over her legs. Orange-veined wings and bodies like black brooches. They have hatched from the ground after incubating for thirteen years – they're as old as the girl, though she doesn't know it. They fill the sky with dark clouds, invading homes, dementing people, destroying new crops. She cannot escape them. The girl tries packing them in pots and pans and boxes; they crawl out from under lids. They sing in the trees, play their tymbals all night. Finally she steals a car, drives though the swarm and out of town. The creatures gather on the windscreen, blinding her. She crashes the car, hides under her coat on the back seat. When she wakes, the plague is gone. The sky is clear. In the ground, in the roots of plants, are soft new eggs.

That book absolutely terrified me, Karolina said, sipping her tea from one of Naomi's fat pottery mugs. *So sinister – their red eyes. And rubbing their abdomens in that creepy way. Such a brilliant metaphor, isn't it, for periodical and sexual threat. In the film, no, they didn't quite manage it. Her vision was completely unforgiving.*

It was disquieting to hear of such an accomplished woman, unknown to me, yet closer to me than anyone. It was moving. Karolina smiled and glanced at the window. The sedge of the fell grass looked very bright, uplit.

What happened to the Cheryl Bone? Is it still here?

We had a ceremonial burning when I left for art school.

Ah, wonderful. Il faut bien que jeunesse se passe. May I see the garden?

Before the taxi arrived to take her to the station, Karolina gave me a bound copy of Naomi's most successful novel, its leather box stitched and rucked, belted delicately with rivets – an item that looked as if it had come from the Florentine Scuola.

This was at the offices. I believe you should have it.

She kissed me goodbye and gave me her number.

Let's stay in touch, Edith. I am looking forward to whatever you make.

The next day, I walked up to the waterfalls. I swam, though the water was bone-shattering and I was no longer impervious. Naomi's ashes blew across the valley like lint and disappeared into low cloud. I thought about the desiccated charcoal in the bags in Shun's workshop, tried to pretend I was not scared, by loneness, my inheritance. I did not contact my father. He had another family; he was a stranger. I'd been raised, capably and neglectfully, by a borrowed woman and her shadow. I lay on Naomi's bed in the empty cottage, comforted by the hollow in her pillow, my face soaked. It was the beginning of grief, for every version of her.

o

Something came together over the following years. I took every opportunity, corporate money I would later regret, met with arts officers and engineers; I hired industrial spaces, kilns, and I salvaged lumber, trying Shun's techniques. We hadn't completed the residency, and I was a wildcard, could experiment, innovate. I could achieve a perfect finish, those suggestive, burnished rivers, and I liked too an unfinished, immolated look. The pieces found recognition. After an exhibition in the Royal Academy, the press picked up on the work, its anomalies and size. The materials and methods suggested an artist either in the vanguard or in crisis. I called Karolina, after which our association was understood.

The designs for Hecky were produced rapidly, in consultation with Sean at Truss Gap. Naomi had been dead three years; her cottage was now a place I would go to plan and think. Looking back, the remit seems impossibly dream-like – an old-style capital spend, the creative allocation of big money, backed by a patron with private land and political heft. They wanted a statement piece by a radical new artist, a landmark on the map. I'd made a contact in the Woodland Trust and arranged the purchase of storm-blown heartwoods from the Caledonian Forest, enormous Scots pine and spruce, protected, listed individually and by century. Hecky's body would be more solid than anything I'd ever worked with.

The trunks arrived on a flatbed at the hired yard and I could hardly believe the girth, the thickness of bark and the heavy shag of remaining foliage. The men in the warehouse next door pinched their rollies to their lips and shook their heads. An extensive health-and-safety check had been carried out, but the project looked like madness. Sean could see exactly the issues, and their cures; he knew how to support the piece, where to anchor it. The site was open, aproned all around by sky and weather, before the

Pennine ascent. There were a million passing cars. He'd calculated mean wind speed, average gusts and catch. He'd even factored the measurements of the Helm Wind, reversed, which never blew from the west.

Nice bit of science fiction, I'm sure it'll help.

Thanks. Maybe give her little tyrannosaurus arms and make my job easier, he joked.

Internal steel poles and a foundation of PFC. Sean had laid marble piers and concrete floors; he'd regenerated and dressed the remotest landscapes, worked in barns and factories with huge water jets and saws. We could prove she was sturdy and safe. Mechanics was not usually the problem, anyway, Sean maintained, finance was – budgets had a way of unstitching, and large works easily stalled. I liked his solutions, his adjustments. He respected every material he worked with, understood their relationships. The casting of brutalist concrete was possible only because of joinery, its brief exoskeleton. He would dig up, label, then replant all the existing gorse on the site.

As we waited in the yard for the convoy of timber, he turned to me.

Do you know how the Cyclone had the steepest drop of any wooden coaster when it was built?

No, I said.

Neither do I. They winged it.

Is that supposed to be funny?

Is what it is. You know the water tables are shifting. She may of course sink.

Right, you're giving me indigestion now.

Hold fast, here they come.

The trucks rumbled in.

I know it. She is the masterwork. A half-burnt assemblage lofting high as a church tower, containing all the unrealistic belligerence and boldness of early ambition. The upper planks of beech were steamed pink, bent and hooped to extraordinary angles, the lower trellis strengthened by charring. She rises above the yellow furze as if from a pyre, hair streaming on the updraft, her back arcing. Welcome North.

Now they are used to her, the low flaccid breasts, the hole between her legs, and sawn gash in her face that seems to scream assent or blow the fire. She's on postcards, aerially shot for local news credits. I've said countless times, she made herself, she stepped out from behind the summits, or rode the lava up. It's true there was a sense of the automatic when I drew her, and that for two years I was in service. It's true too that she was measured, weighed, calculated, again and again, gravitationally, by the millimetre, her keel, her travel, her metrics.

The complaints were immediate and made international news. She was a spectacle, too hazardous to traffic, ugly, indecent – the scorched nipple and obvious vagina. She defined the region fatally. Lady McKenzie defended the piece, unequivocally, chastising prime-time presenters when asked if Hecky would endure or was a folly.

Jonathan, Jonathan. Isn't it time we moved on from all those little white stone cocks. Hurrah for Hecky.

What Ingrid McKenzie believed in was the artistic offence that becomes iconic.

I hadn't known the Scotch Witch was in contention for any award until Karolina called with the news.

Bien joué, darling, you're on the Galeworth list.

Suddenly, there were interviews, documentary requests, dinners and endless fuss. The ceremony itself was excruciating. I had not, I was not, expected to win. When I look at photographs of that evening in the Greenhall, Sean is sitting uncomfortably next to Jonah in a tux. There's a strange downcast creature in a yellow boilersuit dress, doggishly hairstyled, a Japanese tattoo on the shaved strip of bone above her ear. She is so lean she looks armoured. Only Karolina fits – her black hair swept up, an immaculate spine in the backless dress. As soon as the speeches were done, we escaped out the back of the building, with a waiter Jonah had invited, and disappeared into the Underground.

Treen meets Totem.

The New Colossus of British Folk Art.

Karolina was scathing about the profiles.

Folk art? This insufferable boys' club. They can never say a woman is exceptional, better than them.

Soon everything began to feel uncontrollable. I checked my account the week after the ceremony and the figure was stupefying, impossible – I stood at the bank, dumbly staring at the screen while the machine beeped for a decision, then ejected my card.

Do you need help? the man behind me in the queue asked sharply.

Yes, I said.

I reinserted the card, withdrew the maximum daily amount, handed him a stack of notes and walked away.

I was being told who I was but had no sense of it myself. Every time I returned north from some event, and after every interview, I was less sure how I could create. I'd always worked. I worked despite everything difficult, because of difficulty. Now, there was so much money, and opportunity, but for the first time I stopped making.

I walked the city looking for somewhere to hide; walked the riverside, past boat sheds, the old breweries and papermakers. The wicket door of Burntcoat was standing open and an agent was mounting a sign. I asked if I could go in and look. Probate had just been cleared, the family wanted rid of the place quickly, he said. It felt ridiculous to buy such a building, to take on industrial space. At the auction, I was one of two bidders – the other folded almost immediately and wished me luck with the albatross.

I collected the keys, camped in a tent downstairs, on the soft, shit-covered floor. I was stunned by my own stupidity and lay sleeplessly, listening to the pigeons purring in the walls and the plasterwork raining down.

Sometimes it's easier to commit to bad trajectory. There's momentum if not logic. I got rid of my phone, didn't pick up messages from friends or Karolina. In an outbuilding I found an old wooden canoe and every night paddled down to The Anchorman, mooring at the garden railing. The bar was owned by an old schoolmate – Kendra. She remembered me as the bruised-kneed kid I'd been, not the landed artist, and teased me as if the intervening years weren't quite to be believed.

Didn't feel like joining the new century, then, or is this how eccentrics are supposed to travel? I don't have river parking permits.

She was kind, could see something faltering in me. We sat and drank after her shifts, laughing like teenagers, while her husband cleared the glasses and told us to get a grip.

How's the shag-shed? she would ask. *I know you're a country mouse but there used to be insane parties in that building when I first moved here. Total STD hotspot.*

I stayed late into the evening, talking to people in the bar, trying to mask myself, be anonymous. There was dull, pointless sex, like the after-hours business of alley cats. Sometimes Kendra would walk me home, or her husband Nick would drive me, making sure I went in the door and shut it behind me. Sometimes I would paddle back upriver in the darkness, half-cut, the current tugging against the canoe, blind objects slipping past in the water and knocking against the side like skulls.

One night I slipped on the dock and was pulled from the river by passers-by. The memory's vague: swallowing filthy water, a paramedic pumping my chest. Whisky and vomit. I don't know if it was meant or careless. I spent the night in hospital, was given precautionary antibiotics. Every rib ached. There were reports in the press. One journalist tracked me to the building, lingered a few days, approaching when I exited and trying to get me to talk, extract a confession, maybe. The piece he wrote was nasty and researched; I was a fraud, a madwoman's daughter. He cited Kokoschka, compared me not to the artist of giant scale and genius but to the tragic doll, the fake wife. I began saying stupid things to friends, saying I would give up, retrain.

Jonah arrived at Burntcoat after I'd called him drunk and told him the little blue boat of my soul had capsized.

Do you remember what other nonsense you said to me, jou malkop? he demanded. He took me by the shoulders and shook me, then threw his bag into a corner and looked around.

I'm going to squat in your palace awhile, princess. Capeesh? Where's the latrine?

The first day he got up early, coughing, cursing. I made tea on the camp stove and Jonah began to shovel piles of bird shit from the corners. There were calcified oyster shells and crabs' legs, pats of mystery compost, ledgers we couldn't decipher in the cupboards. He was between gigs, he said, low on funds, and needed something to keep him out of trouble; maybe he'd photograph the renovation, me, teach himself to plumb and parquet.

Just like the old days, he said. *Except I'm going bald and you're the next Rodin, apparently.*

We'd got on well together in the collective after college; Jonah was enormously talented, full of ideas, and usually lovelorn, too distracted by beauty, he said – there was always a tragic affair being conducted. We both knew he was shoring me up, that I'd touched a nerve. His father was a suicide, had shot himself in the stomach with his duty gun – the maid had found him moments before Jonah arrived back from school; she'd covered his torso, called for medical assistance, but hadn't managed to clean the wall. Jonah understood shame, anger, the insidious repetitions of example; he'd told the story to everyone.

The old bastard was still alive when I came in; he asked me if I'd got homework to do.

He helped create Burntcoat. He spoke to the glaziers – assured them the vast window measurements were correct, hefted a reclaimed bath up the stairs with me, and the cast-iron stove that seemed heavier than a planet. We set our sore backs against the wall.

There's a reason no one in their right mind wanted this ruddy behemoth. But you still need more space if you're going to play mega-Lego in here. You need to get rid of that.

He pointed at the building's middle wall. There was a casual discussion about whether it was load-bearing. We worked with sledgehammers, taking out the stone with wild swings, unpacking the building's light and length, not knowing if the entire structure would collapse on us. He fetched his camera, stood unobtrusively, splay-legged, assessing the glint off the river. The shutter scraped closed at the perfect moment with the sound of a struck match. My arm was caught in its blurred motion like a piece of equipment, an explosive burst of sun behind it.

At night we cooked on a camping stove or ate at The Anchorman.

You're not off the hook, he told me, *this isn't work.*

I held up a calloused, grazed hand.

Feels like work to me.

No, they didn't buy you with that dirty corporate cash.

Will you let me pay you?

You can buy me another beer and my ticket back home when we're done.

You're going back to Cape Town? I didn't think you would.

What we couldn't do we enlisted builders to complete. Money drained out of the account. The roof, the flooring, the heating, tiles. For the workspace, a lathe, saws, clamps and compressors, the Bullfinch torches – I would no longer have to work off site. We sourced industrial scaffolding so models could be constructed in the yard, and towards the end of the renovation Jonah set it up outside the building and began to write on the brickwork. I didn't really know what he was doing until I climbed up to the platform and saw he was holding a copy of The Reddening in one hand, transcribing it in white masonry paint.

You're on chapter eight?

Ja.

Burntcoat became some kind of chimerical home, the studio below, an upcycled bare-brick apartment above, two hemispheres, both me.

There are friends in life who save us then disappear from sight. They remain indelible in the heart. I went to

Jonah's wedding fifteen years ago and, though we speak on videocalls, I've not seen him since. Before he left, he insisted we have a party. We strung lights in the yard, set up a stereo system and invited everyone. Kendra arrived with several kegs. The music rang round the empty riverside and drew people over as if it were a concert. There were burning drums full of petrol and wood. I ended up with a woman called Ro, testing my boundaries, she said, which she didn't seem to mind.

I've been responsible for loads of switches, she told me proudly. *You have extraordinary skin.*

She was clever, worked for a housing charity; she was horrified that I owned Burntcoat and kept propane under the apartment. We danced and kissed, went upstairs to use the bathroom. Jonah waved at me.

Is he your boyfriend?

He's my Huckleberry.

She had heavy breasts, and pale-pink, almost disappearing nipples when she pulled off her vest, a stud in her tongue. She'd brought pills.

What is that?

It's jade. Don't worry. Open wide.

The green pellet dissolved to chalk, tasted of aspirin and zinc. After half an hour I led her to the bedroom. She'd been in similar situations before. She slowed it down. Her compliments were half political, designed to reassure and educate. She loved this part here, and here.

Feel for yourself, it's so incredibly soft.

She sucked gently, as if I were a man, opened me, pushed her tongue inside, then her fingers. When she took her hand away I felt empty, incomplete. The warm metal stud clicked on her teeth, felt like a tiny knuckle wherever she used it. I was full of fireworks; light kept sparking in my head, my pelvis, between the discs of my spine. Every touch was like static, gorgeous, too much.

You should stay on this side, Edith.

OK. Sure.

She moved on to someone else after that night, but for those minutes and hours it seemed perfect. Downstairs, Jonah was dancing, bare-chested, unsynchronised, and everything around him was vivid and over-defined. Then there was a secondary phantom shape hovering beside him, and shapes beside the tanks of flame, the people moving in the shadows, a couple fucking upright on the fire escape. I could still feel Ro's tongue.

At some point Jonah went to the balcony window above the river, opened it and stepped out. On the dock, people looked up, and Ro pointed.

Your Huckleberry?

He was standing naked, immaculate and still, his head cast down towards the water, like a heron, a saint. A few people clapped and whistled, as if the appearance was the performance. I knew he was going to jump. I knew Jonah, his reasons and reasonless commitments, his need for contrast. The river was deep and permissive, but its bed was planted with hidden wreckage.

He stood for a moment, put a foot on the shallow rail and pulled back, then launched himself outwards. I can still see it. His body in the air, a rigid human star, suspended, luminous in the building's light, then dropping fast, his penis sailing upward, his fists clenched. Dark water exploded as he hit. He disappeared and waves gnashed against the sidings and the dock. I heard Ro exclaim,

No fucking way.

The shout when he surfaced was feral, half injured, half exalted. He tossed his head, swam to the dock. People cheered and jumped into the water. The party had been baptised. The police arrived within an hour.

But I saw, and I still see, a different version too, like the twin shapes the drug created. Jonah jumps and rides the air. The surface of the river closes over and the ripples calm. He sinks underneath, shedding oxygen in a long dry stream, and enters the serrated bed of the river. Beside old hulls and rusting motors, between the curtains of reeds, he stands, mouth open and flooded, his ankles wrapped in chain.

The bad wake of the pill, or the gravity-defying act, months of labour and adrenaline. The vast space where Naomi had been, into which my monster had risen. Whatever the trigger, I spent the rest of the night in quiet crisis in the yard, with Ro stroking my back, telling me no one had died, everything was fine, breathe, breathe. Blue lights bouncing over the river gave everyone enough time to disperse. The penalty fine is still pinned up in the kitchen, next to the original prints of Jonah's photo series, Mind-House, like some kind of severance notice.

o

It might take a lifetime to know how to live. How it's all made meaningful or tolerable, how to attain some semblance of wisdom. I've tried methods of accommodation and acceptance. Not being delighted or repelled by the world, by how it presents. Trying to see inside. To find essence, which is benign. I've travelled, walked pilgrim routes and all the mountains of the north, heading up into the fells in a solitary, fatal way. I've fasted and meditated. The year I turned fifty, I spent several months in South-East Asia. In Thailand I found a group. The leader's name was Subhadassi, he was kind and had no sense of pity whatsoever. His small jokes in the morning confused the few Western participants. I tried to be as neither man nor woman, nor an artist. The robes were loose and rough, like rust wings; my identity was folded into a bag and left beside the pallet bed. We collected water to wash and drink, burnt coils of incense, repeated mantras. For several weeks I sat watching a corpse decompose. We continued living, talking, meditating with the grey blossoming presence among us.

This too is part of existence, Subhadassi told me. *Meuan-gan.*

At any given moment the body is simply its state: reformation and decay of flesh, its neutral routes. There was a sensuality – unfrightening, comforting even – of cells altering hour by hour. Not like I remembered, or perhaps exactly the same, and I was being altered, my concept of existence. It is immunity to change that we struggle to accomplish, that seems so inhuman and freeing. Something intrudes, ego, repetitions of the past, or small hard fears, like deposits in the kidney, the breast. The awareness of suffering or desire, hope, an unprovable beyond. I tried these things, but the noise in my head would not stop, would always begin again, on the plane, on the descent from the clouds, every emotion and failing leaking in through the cracks in the air. The body is a wound, a bell ringing in emergency – life, life, life.

The virus has shed its older names. They were frightening, incorrect, discriminatory. Hanta. Nova. Now it is simply AG3. It is contained, an event in a previous era from which we continue to learn. Contingency planning. Social tracking. Herd control. The picture of the pathogen – orange and reticulated – has become as recognisable as the moon. Children sketch it in science lessons, the curious arms, proteins and spikes. The civic notices listing symptoms, and the slogans, look vintage.

It's probably here, you said at the start of that year, and you were right. It had been mistaken in the hospitals as something virulent and seasonal. One. Then dozens, fifty, a hundred. This is how the count starts – gradually, exponentially, numbers that insist on belief, and eventually confound it.

I was eating dinner in the restaurant and waiting for you to finish work when the announcement came. There were only two customers. You'd been watching your phone for bulletins as you worked. I was watching mine. The prime minister, live, apologetic, firm as a disappointed parent, told the nation to go home, and stay home: everything would close. She was declaring a national state of emergency. You stopped, glanced up, held my eyes. You finished making a dish, boxed it and handed it to the waiting customers, who took the free meal and said something about strange times. The phrase we would all use, again and again, until it was devoid of meaning. Then you walked to the door and turned the sign.

o

I have this feeling – of being unplugged and too far from the socket and what remains is a red warning bar. I've been out in the city, but it was too much and drained me. It might be the last time. There are different accounts about resurgence. It's quicker, more painful, in some ways kinder. It's a dragged-out, incremental affair, and patients pray for it to be over.

Rostam had the tree ready when I went to collect it. It was wrapped in paper at the base, and waiting at the back of the flower stall. Among the bright leaves were small knuckles of blossom, one or two of the flowers had sprung free. Just as I'd asked. There was no ebullience when Rostam saw me. He nodded. His hat was sitting back on his head in a felt halo, like a jazz musician's, the hair underneath grey, cropped very short. How quickly it all passes, I thought. The colours of the tulips seemed aggressively bright, flares of red, purple, yellow. My eyes felt very sensitive and my head was beginning to hurt. I'd brought the small, wheeled truck I use in the workshop, and I parked it beside the hut.

Even from two open buds, the fragrance was strong. I inhaled, closed my eyes. Rostam took money from a customer and then came over. With his little finger he pointed to the white inside the greenery.

Just arriving, he said. *Is it correct?*
Yes. Thank you.
How are you?
I'm quite tired.
I understand, he said. *Would you like some tea?*
It was a kind offer, something beyond trade.
Go and sit inside, please, he urged, *go and sit.*

I began to put on my mask, but he stopped me, saying it was not necessary. Inside the booth were two chairs, a small chrome kettle, glasses, sugar. A packet of cigarettes and a packet of mints. The wood of the booth smelled of pollen and greenery, decades of stock. There was a photograph on the wall of Rostam's family, his son and daughter dressed in the city's football colours, his wife. A beaded blue-glass eye hung above the picture, similar to the one you had on the door of the restaurant.

Rostam came inside, poured the tea, his leather coat creaking as he leant forward to pass me a glass. We sat for a few minutes quietly. The small, elegant rituals. It reminded me of you and I wondered if he would mention your name. It's so long since I've heard it spoken.
Do you have everything you need? he asked.
I think so.
Good. Good.
Thank you for finding the tree.

94

Of course. It was only a short drive. My son came with me for company.

Rostam sipped tea from his glass.

I am thinking of retiring.

Will your son take over the stall?

No, he wants to study medicine. My wife would like to move to Antakya. She misses her mother.

Will you go? I asked.

Perhaps. We have a small house there.

You've done so well here. You've been in the market longer than anyone now.

The council kept my old rates. I have a different status, you know. They call me Rosty.

Yes.

My friends have been leaving for years. For me it doesn't matter, my country doesn't exist any more.

I nodded.

I remember.

I remember too, Rostam said. *I don't want to remember. You'll be missed if you go.*

He laid a hand on mine.

You and I, we're just one mountain apart.

The tea was sweet, strong. My breakfast that morning had been tiny and tasted of nothing. I thanked Rostam again. As I stood I felt unsteady and he offered to deliver the tree later that day, but I told him I was fine, could manage – this is my tendency. Carefully, he lifted the tree onto the truck, made sure it would not tip. I went to pay him but he held up a hand.

No. Please. We cannot.

I tried to insist but he shook his head, looked pained, slightly offended. So I accepted the gift and thanked him again. As I was leaving the stall, he called out to me,

Safaret bekheir.

I turned back, but he was looking the other way, already speaking to another customer.

The tree shook and juddered as the truck rattled along the streets, down past the cathedral to the river. My arms felt weak, and I was desperate to get home. I did not have my glasses or my Peltors. People were looking at me. They do look at me. My hair is long now, almost as long as Naomi's was, but grey. All my clothes are too big and slightly foolish. I belt the waists with cord and keep sewing the cardigans. There are no mirrors in Burntcoat any more, I took them down after you, so I don't know exactly how I appear. I believe I must look ill, with that odd solid translucence of wax, and the tenderised motions.

I was exhausted when I got home, could barely carry the pot up the stairs to the apartment. I could feel my heart stabbing away. Stubbornness has always made me push myself too far. I kicked open the door, managed to get through. Suddenly I felt overwhelmed. I slumped on the floor and the tree dropped, went over on its side, the soil scattering everywhere. I found myself unable to get up, disorientated. My breath was flurrying in panic, and the roaring noise filled my head as if a faint was coming. I lay on my side, tried to get air to my lungs, tried to think rationally. But from nowhere I heard myself shouting.

Fuck you, fuck you, I am not doing this yet!

And I began crying, the unrestrained sobs of a powerless child.

My old blue jacket from Japan was hanging on the peg by the door. It is indigo, I thought. It still fits, and I can stand and put it on, I can stand and put it on. I stared hard at the material, the braided fastenings down the front, and counted backwards from two thousand, as if coming down the steps of a shrine, until the noise and the hysterics passed.

o

You arrived at Burntcoat with a bag of clothes, some books, a few valued possessions. After the announcement you stayed late in the restaurant, moving stock between refrigerators and freezers, turning off power. You went home and packed. Among the things you brought was an antique brass coffee grinder that had been your grandfather's. It was slender, very beautiful, had been manufactured in a more artful, mechanical age.

Sorry if it smells like pepper. My grandfather used it for the corns as well.

I put it in a prominent place on the kitchen counter, as if to mark its worth, which was really your worth. We hadn't discussed your coming. It seemed obvious.

Let me make one for you.
Thanks. I like my coffee peppery, please.
Of course.

You tipped in the beans, fitted it together, wound the handle at the top. The grinder took patience to produce enough grains. But now we had time. The restaurant was shut. The streets were emptying. We were entering a suspended zone.

My grandfather wanted me to have his name, you said as you turned the handle.
What does it mean?
You thought for a moment.
No end?
Endless.
Yes, endless.
And Edith?

To be trapped with a lover is a boon; it has the intensity of a dream. This is what I thought, those first days. I'd lived with a man only once before. Your presence was different; allied. The shock of another human nearby when one expects to be alone. The strangeness of a shirtless back, that plate of muscle from spine to shoulder that seems wrongly wingless. In the first week of confinement, we spent hours in bed, deferring the sex, luxuriating in the long mutilation of desire, or eating, or talking, or reading by the stove.

Are you worried?

About what?

The restaurant.

Yes. What can I do?

It had been years since you'd finished a book. You read in English, slowly, your head bent over in sombre concentration, like an executioner's. You tidied the yard, cooked for us. There had been a run on the supermarkets and rationing of products was under way. But we had supplies from the restaurant, a cache, and there was no sense of panic. You tried calling your family often; the lines were busy, or the connection stalled, overloaded.

We learnt each other, domestically. It was like a hastily arranged marriage. We sat on the little balcony talking, watching the river transport colours and the occasional swan. There was no screaming from the school playgrounds. No traffic. A mute sky.

It's amazing, all the birdsong. So quickly they've taken over.

A republic of birds.

Don't you think the air feels different?

Clearer?

Yes.

The cathedral bells were not being tolled by staff but were running automatically – minor-key refrains repeating every hour. The chiming was exact, eerie in the lack of human syncing.

I don't like that, I confessed.

What don't you like?

The bells – it sounds like a death knell.

Knell? I don't know that word.

When someone dies, they ring three church bells. They have different names. For the stages of death, I think.

You nodded. Perhaps you already knew.

In Islam they call the Friday sela. Then they say who has died. Before it's too late, pray. Death finds all of us. We came from Allah, we go to Allah. Every creature will taste death.

You tutted and looked up.

I don't like that. It's to scare us, make us behave.

Are you scared?

Are you?

No. I think we would know by now. If we had it.

Your eyes in exterior light became greyer, clearer; in photographs their colour can hardly be seen. It seemed you were a different creature outside.

We planted tomatoes in the yard, pretending we were on an island. People our age were sick. The stronger the immune system, the worse the fight when it turned against the host. It was so hard to believe, when our bodies were flourishing. The city was very quiet, but faintly, in the distance, we could hear sirens on the main road to the hospital.

No one knew how long confinement would go on, how long we would be cooped up, how long society would be shut down. I didn't mind. I thought about Naomi's cottage at the end of the valley, the weeks of packed snow, shovelling a path to the car and the hard black ice underneath that meant, even in thaw, the road was still too lethal to drive.

All the strange, secret behaviour that was now allowed, could flourish behind the barricades. Creative, restive acts, pastimes run amok, violence. There'd been a rush on pet-buying, and already animals were being dumped as the reality and expense of care became too much.

I'd like a dog, I told you. *Where I come from everyone had dogs.*

Are you serious?

Your expression was dark, disapproving, I thought.

You want one now? you asked.

Yes.

Are you absolutely sure?

It was a joke, Halit.

You shouldn't joke about those things.

I looked at you, confused. Had I hit a nerve? We were about to have our first silly argument, and over nothing, animals, status symbols, ownership, I did not understand what. You sniffed the air loudly, once, twice. Then you dropped to your knees and went forward onto your hands. You began to walk on all fours, smelling the table, my feet, the floor. The total lack of inhibition took a moment to process.

Oh, I see.

You barked, padded back to me and I started laughing.

Yes, I get it.

You barked again, walked to the door and scratched it, whined. The impression was remarkably good, far too earnest. I felt a hot, embarrassed blush on my neck.

OK, OK, stop. Get up.

You let your tongue hang out, stared at me with remedial, slavish eyes. Then you howled and scratched at the floor. I had to play along.

What do you want, dog? To go out?

You shook your head.

Come in?

You came to me obediently, sniffed my knees. You licked my shins, nipped at the wool socks I was wearing.

Hey! Stop that! That's bad.

You whined, chastised, then began to lick my legs again, the knees, higher.

Oh my God, you have to stop now. Please.

Your head disappeared under my cotton shirt; the sensation changed, long strokes of the tongue. Your hands slid up to my buttocks, under the thin cotton underwear, and the game dissolved, became human. You pulled the cotton to the side, breathed warmly. I pulled up the shirt so I could see you, then unbuttoned it and threw it on the floor. Your tongue was like a soft wet razor, sharpening at the tip, drawing itself again and again along a soft strop. I put my hands in your hair, tried to steady myself. Your sounds were human now.

Can we go to the bed?

You didn't reply. The air felt too thin to hold me upright. You pulled me down on the floor, positioned me in front, clasped hold, curled over my back and began. If we went deep enough into each other, there would be a hiding place.

o

The images are so strong from that time. The nurse standing in the empty aisle, her back to us, hair dishevelled and her uniform crumpled, the weight of the shopping basket, though it is empty, pulling her body downwards. The Pope, kneeling in the rain in a deserted St Peter's Square. Cuban volunteer doctors exiting the plane in Naples, where a variant has become unstoppable, their faces like bronze casts, the hands of the airport workers frozen mid-applause. And a plane full of equipment sitting on the runway at Heathrow, its cargo door closing, caught in some snare of bureaucracy. The Welsh doctor who has cut the bottom off a large water cooler and placed it over his head as a mask – ripples in the plastic amplifying the ripples in his brow; he would be among the first medical staff to die.

I've looked at those images often, the spontaneous moments – which seem to frieze history, to make it, in a fixed moment, epic, still kinetic. It is chance. Or the gift of the photographer to predict, to respond. Jonah would say, there is skill, but it's luck, there's no eye faster than fate. Frame by frame, it is all caught. Now. We are afraid. Now. We are suffering. Now. Our devastation begins.

And the images later – I look at those too – of hastily built warehouses for patients; they are hangars not hospices, their ranks of beds untended. An aerial shot of cars snaking up to the hospital gates, doors open, people emerging to assess the delay, and, so tiny in the picture that she might be missed, a woman is running, past the cars, with a body slung over her shoulder. She is insectile, strong as an ant.

Now. We are no longer human. Now. We fight unambiguously, to save, to survive.

Ambulances parked in a tight row across the entrance of the hospital, dark-screened, ready to be deployed, or unmanned and shouldered close like bulls, like soldiers. Military vehicles on the streets, a single pedestrian passing an armed unit, not looking up, no longer surprised by the deadly presence of guns.

We closed our eyes but our minds still made images. There were lurid quarantine dreams. Yours were immigrant's anxiety, the guilt of separation written up in the long reel of night. Your family, one by one, were executed. The civil war, so long feared by everyone, was declared by your subconscious, and you were drafted. Your mother was always sick, bleeding internally, her skin tallow as a candle, or your father was missing: he'd been taken back across the border, shot in the Crazy Forest. I heard you mumbling in your sleep, your fists clenched over your chest, the blood seeping back in your arms. In the morning your fingers would be numb – it would take half an hour for sensation to return. Sometimes you ticked like a clock in your sleep, tiny jerks, your breath apnoeic. I pressed your shoulder, tried to turn you without waking. You spoke in the half-state, moving up through languages as you woke.

Ne. Sağol, sorry. There was a bus collecting us . . .

The close heat of our bodies was a hothouse for nightmares.

In mine I was afloat again. Burntcoat had come loose from the bank and was drifting, rushing towards black falls, or pitching up colossal ripping waves in an ocean.

I dreamt of a little girl. Her body was a previous version of mine – sculpted shoulder blades, a fast heart jumping visibly under the skin like a frog's, one of her eyes slightly hooded. She had pale, copperish hair. I didn't tell you about her at first, in case you thought it was some proposition. She came unprovoked. I was, I've always been, ambivalent about children. But I dreamt of this girl so often that for a few weeks she seemed like our child. She was so clear to me. Sitting at the table drawing, absorbed completely by the rub on the page. Little milk teeth inside big gums, her hair spilling finely from its fastening. That reduced palette of facial expressions; moods seeming, in children, so categorical. She would run between rooms in her underpants, her body lean and gleaming, the soft tummy sucking in and out like bellows. Its navel was missing – she was unborn.

Finally, I told you about her. You were charmed – I'd not learnt yet that men from your country possess incautious joy towards children. You hadn't been raised with the recoil of English boys.

We should give her a name, you said.

OK.

You thought about it.
How about Hülya?
That's a nice name.
It means dream.
You would even ask me in the mornings.
Did you see Hülya? What did she do?
She was in the bath. She was putting hairs from the drain onto a bar of soap, very carefully. She was making a picture with them.

The girl didn't speak. She gnawed at my curiosity. I've never believed in muses. But I thought about trying to make her in the studio, a kind of prop project – the fable commission had stalled. I needed more propane for the Bullfinches but there was nowhere to get it. She should be life-size, something I'd never really tried, and greenwood, maybe. When I began her, the idea corrupted. I saw scarecrows in the field, brittle straw hair. Ugly hessian sea-dollies, stitched with holes in their crotches by sailors, passed around below deck, absorbent enough to relieve half the crew.

Under such circumstances, the pressure of love and catastrophe, the mind breaks a little, spills its mysteries and confidences. I understand psychological theory. In therapy I was once asked to select random objects and make a map of the people in my life, deceased and alive.

The symbolism and positioning would have meaning, help me visualise and reveal my tendency.

Do it without thinking too much, the therapist said. *It doesn't have to be art.*

I must have looked at her sceptically, that turpentine look, which, I've been told, strips people.

I understand there have been a lot of casualties, she said. *But let's give it a go.*

Leaves, rocks, sea glass. Lego people, badges, bric-a-brac. Souvenirs, junk: all of it could be vested with association. Naomi and I: wooden peg dolls tied with string. At the edge of the relief, a father, headless, plastic. A few friends and colleagues, scattered and assorted. I chose you last, the eye-shaped, silver-worked agate, sat it on top of a mirror. I stood and looked down at the constellation I'd made, tried, when the therapist asked, to explain the meaning and coordinates, the spaces between.

Do you feel any guilt?
    Maybe.
    How do you feel about your condition?
    Which one.
    Who is this, Edith?
    Both of them.

It's a simple exercise, in which we see and read our small, inconsequential lives, and realise we are, in part, curator.

It's all art, even thought, everything is. What we make is made of not only the self but a thousand other naive or rarefied versions. I was left alone with my hands, my impulses. I've pulled from myself all manner of binary things, constructed them in spaces where they belong without assignment, brute, interpretable figures in the landscape. Those are not my children. Hecky is not mine. I'm responsible for her creation but can't say what she is or isn't. A talisman for travellers. Some prehistoric female conduit. All the women punished for deviance, for capacity: women who were put to the fire, who blackened, became mutant, and got up from the pyre, inoculated. There is the mother, but when there is no definite mother something else emerges through its own cunt, with genes that are destructed and more resilient. I can't say I wasn't prepared.

o

At art school, students were inducted into all the workshops – metalwork and wood, the darkrooms and studio spaces. We could use them whenever we wanted, in theory. Few women took up metal and laser-cutting, and by the end of the year I was the only one left. I'd experimented with painting for a while, which was fashionable; my drafting was good, but I always wanted to step behind the canvas. For a while I sourced vellum, painted on both sides and built images outwards, tricking dimension. My classmates frowned and recoiled.

It's no worse than your leather shoes, I said.

Naomi had handwritten The Reddening on ordinary brown baking paper, long scrolls of it, then had paid the typist. It suited her new language, I think, the physical aspect of dysphasia, though seemed also a mix of material prudence and disinvestment. The manuscript process was very difficult. The typist accepted the rolls, grudgingly. She didn't like the story, or thought it was an amateur's novel, a waste of money. When we arrived at the house to collect chapters, she would hand over the stack and squint behind her Fresnel lenses.

Surely this unfortunate girl has a name? I may have missed it somewhere in the text.

She doesn't have a name, Naomi told her again.

Oh, what an unusual thing. Might I ask, why aren't there any adults to help her?

Because it's her story. There are no adults.

Gracious!

In the workshop, the machines were old. The spaces were shabby and had the smell of grease and filings. The morning lectures were interesting and progressive enough, but they were disconnected from the misogyny of practice, the manliness of history. It was the technicians, not the lecturers, who were the real teachers, the keepers of knowledge.

There was a limit to what a woman was expected to achieve. Once, I overheard a discussion about my work: I was just doing it to prove a point. One or two instructors were glad of the genuine interest. I worked with a blacksmith called Carlo. Even the boys considered his field antiquated, too agricultural. Carlo was small and compact. Under his shredded jumpers he seemed more like a chimney sweep than the proverbial village ironmonger. Smithing required more stamina than strength, he said.

I liked it – the forced grace of elements in a molten, malleable state, a craft that felt earned. Work at the furnace was tedious, sweaty and hard, but it was distracting. I didn't have to think about how I didn't fit in. The other students were rapidly pairing and getting flats together, competing in levels of squalor; one or two were getting pregnant and acting like a baby was just another creative experience. They drank and smoked, went to raves, missed class. I was four hours away from Naomi and the cottage, and reeked of innocent competence.

Through Carlo I met my first boyfriend. Ali worked in the art school, had once been a student but was now a kind of go-to man for stock and transport, as well as dope and tickets to local gigs. He hung out with the first-years, flirted puppyishly with the girls and developed churlish camaraderie with the boys. His looks were beautiful and slightly repellent, feminine, almost lecherous: hazel eyes, their colour noosed around large pupils, a smooth full mouth. He applied Vaseline from a small yellow tin every night. His head was shaved at the sides and Brylcreemed, he wore laced boots even in summer, an orange-and-black National Coal Board jacket – homage to an era of dead labour movements. People recognised him across campus, the dropout socialist. His car, a cheap white Escort, always ran at a quarter-tank or less, the petrol light endlessly flicking on.

I agreed to let him shave my head too. He said I would look like a particular French actress he liked who was sexy, tough – famous for the opening credits of a film where a man is going down on her. I watched the curled tresses slither to the ground.

There she is. Shall I do anywhere else?

Ali was from the south; he teased me about my inexperience, called me E. He knew how to gently undermine and make himself seem heroic, while submitting to moods of bitter disappointment. The half-filled sketchbooks and aborted poems. The bar stories, which were better than the experiences. He could strum the basic chords of protest songs on a guitar, would take off his shirt while playing, his skin unblemished and sallow, both nipples pierced. I didn't understand his interest in me, didn't understand that jealousy loves to keep wounding itself.

There are periods of self-mutilation in youth, experiments with identity; mine have been in liminal spaces, between loss and success. We lived together in his flat. It was damp, nearly windowless, the lower half of a house on a main road near the racetrack. There had been a lot of other women, I understood. He believed in me, he said.

The sex was unemotional, schooling, gradually lacking foreplay; after straight-seeming congress he wanted to wear certain clothes, nylon tights that held the bulge. He found it difficult to climax, needed pressure, which brought me pain. He asked me to take the pill; it made me feel hormonally unaligned, slightly crazed. The first shaving joke had been serious. He liked depilation, told me to hold still and trust him as the clippers buzzed.

I spent hours trying to understand the situation, to predict when he would be loving or callous, and comprehend why. Why tenderness became rough. Why I endured it. One infection travelled up to my kidneys. I spent three days in a fever, passing blood, before he drove me to the student clinic.

You're making a lot of fuss, E. Everyone gets them.

Suffering was universal, Ali said – it was the only thing that kept people levelled. He liked Blake, Courbet, de Sade. I knew he was wrong. I'd watched my mother climb back up from ruin, hobbling against physiotherapists, releasing and holding her urine, exercising her jaw and her tongue. But I listened to the theories and stayed the course. There were subtle warnings from Carlo, issued to me when I seemed quiet and troubled, if I'd arrived too early at college.

Know where your boundary is, that's all I'm saying. These pieces know what they're doing. I see a lot of wannabes but there's no glory in a lifestyle.

Ali was scathing of students who sold works in their final degree shows.

Look at that pretentious shit with the price tag.

In front of others, he would play proud, deferential.

E is a genius, she works like a navvy, twice as talented as I ever was.

To me he said, *it's going to look hysterical if you try anything bigger.*

Though she was largely insensitive, Naomi hated Ali. I could see the signs, the breakdown in her safe behaviours, phrases she would not normally have used. Ali despised his own family and often came to the cottage when I visited, though he complained about the narrow, unmade road over the moors, called the house *Arse-end-dale.*

He was interested in Naomi, her unusualness, her programming, the fact that she'd been an author. Her fallen status appealed on several levels; he spoke to her as if they were equals and made her tense and disorganised. His bare-chested presence in the small kitchen, the silver rings shining in their softly erect beds, his ashtrays and spreadeagled ease. Alpha displays. She'd not had a man in her domain since my father – even after I'd left home.

Every week she and I wrote to each other; Ali thought it ridiculous.

What could she possibly have to say? She only sees the fucking squirrels. She doesn't even have a telly.

She's not very good with that kind of light.

Riiiight.

Naomi was still teaching, subsisting meanly. He would ask her about writing, test her, reading old copies of her novels at night by the fire, then questioning why a character had said this or that.

I don't remember, Alistair. It was written a long time ago.

She never asked him what he'd accomplished, or what he hoped to, and the assumption of permanent failure was clear.

Why does she always hum under her breath like that?

It helps her concentrate.

Why does she want to be in the middle of nowhere?

It makes her feel safe.

Safe?

When he really wanted to stir, he asked,

Have you never thought about seeing your dad?

I made the mistake of telling Ali what had happened to her, the whole story. It's true she had become odder, her face often froze in startlement when someone spoke to her, and there were habitual tics. She wore the same clothes day after day, and the big shabby velvet housecoat; sometimes she put one of the quails in the gown's pocket to warm it. She walked outside barefoot, her heels cracked, her toes hooked and red. Ali tried to goad and gaslight her.

It is Tuesday today, isn't it, Naomi? For a minute I thought I'd gone mad.

It's Wednesday, Alistair. We take the bins up to the milkstand on Tuesdays.

Wednesday, Wednesday, right. Thanks.

Naomi would use my full name immediately after Ali had called me by his nickname.

Edith, can you pass me the butter?

We were in my old bedroom, one wall's span from Naomi's head. I don't know why I let him do the things he did there. For years she and I had protected ourselves, but I let him in.

One morning, while we were alone in the kitchen, she turned to me.

Why does he eat the dark, Edith?

Sorry? What do you mean?

There was always that potential for glitch, but in this instance Naomi had nailed it.

Eating the dark. Yes. That's what he does. Eating it, and shitting it out on everyone. Do you enjoy it too?

She was looking directly at me in her guileless way. I avoided her eyes.

I don't know what you mean. I think you're confused.

She set two bowls and two spoons on the table. Every time I had to add the third and tell myself, habit, it's just habit. I went to the cupboard to get another dish and spoon, expecting the usual phrase to follow, *Thank you, I can stand.* Instead she slowly tipped the chair at Ali's setting backwards, and it thumped and clattered on the stone floor.

OK, Edith. Why don't you draw me a picture of how I should feel about Ali.

I was stunned. The tone, the sarcasm – I didn't know her capable of it any more. It was so rare that anything broke the surface. I was angry, ashamed, unwilling to admit my bad choices. Now, now that I'm independent and don't need her, I thought, she's acting like my mother?

Ali and I left a day early, in a fug of hostility, with Naomi staring hard at me, as if I might still answer her question.

On the drive back, Ali kept shaking his head and blowing air through his nose.

Fucking nonsense was that. Just grow up, the pair of you.

The relationship swiftly began to fall apart. Ali went out drinking, didn't come home. He began to speak to me in a way I knew was over the line.

You're acting like a paranoid cunt. I just need some space.

I was filled with anxiety. There were nights when I was sure Naomi was dead, that the call would come in the morning. I would lie, paralysed, crying silently next to Ali. I stopped taking the pill and my periods went haywire. I stopped writing letters to my mother. The things I was making at the furnace with Carlo were disturbing and compelling, pushing the possible scale. My tutors commended the ideas, began to take the work seriously exactly as I began to fall apart.

There was a day I came back to the flat early from college and found the door bolted inside. I knocked but there was silence. I knocked again, called to Ali to let me in. I thought I heard a thud, a window sash lifting or something being set down heavily on a table. The door remained shut. I banged harder. A cold feeling trickled into me. He was with someone; I knew it. Another girl from the art school – the intuition was inexplicable but I was suddenly sure. Her name was Helena. I barely knew her but she'd been smiling at me, asking how I was, complimenting my portfolio. She was slender-chested with pixie hair and a tattoo of her father's air-force number on her shoulder. Exactly, authentically what Ali would like. I kept pounding, my fist going numb. Then I stood quietly, waiting, imagining them continuing behind the locked door, her small breasts nipped between his fingers.

I found him later in one of the city's pubs, not a student haunt but an old man's drinking hole, a hideaway. It was November; I was soaked and freezing cold, had searched hours for him, asking who had seen him. Carlo had finally told me. Ali accused me of being insane. I shoved him against the bar while the punters stared, followed him outside, shouting that he was a liar. He pushed me over in the street, was arrested and spent the night in a cell. Then he went to find Helena. It seemed impossible we would continue, that I'd ever put the needle back in.

A day later I developed pain in my lower abdomen, and the watery brown blood of the past few weeks became fast and bright red. I walked to the medical centre, vomited on the floor and collapsed. An ambulance was called. The pregnancy was ectopic and rupturing. When I woke, I'd been catheterised and was wearing a morphine belt. The incision was weeping into its bandage, had been hastily closed. The fallopian tube was irreparable and had been removed.

Ali was sitting by the bed. His face was pitiful, an expression of sorrow almost operatic. He wanted to look after me, he said, make amends, come home with me for Christmas. He tried to thaw the atmosphere, talked about announcing an engagement that had never been proposed. I played dead, agreed, pretended to sleep. I didn't press the anaesthetic button, letting the pain mount. When the nurse removed the drain I started screaming, had to be held on the bed.

After I was discharged, I spent a week at the flat, limping to the toilet, dozing, trying to focus. I'd been prescribed sedatives but hadn't broken the seal on the box. Ali attended to me then left me alone; I was sure he was still fucking her, and I knew I'd reached the end. When I was able, I packed a bag of clothes and left it under the bed. I took a bus to the college and told Carlo I was dropping out. He sat me down.

No, you're bloody not. Just take a longer holiday. Get pissed with your mates. I'll swing it with the department – no one else is getting a distinction.

The wound in my side ached and stung sharply as the nerves knit together. I wrote to Naomi, told her where to be and when – the walk to the postbox felt like the most important thing I had ever done in my life. Two days later, when Ali had left for work, I took a taxi to the station, got on the train and hunkered in a seat in the furthest carriage. I didn't breathe properly until we shuddered forward, began passing bridges and tenements. A woman sitting nearby in the carriage smiled and asked,

Is it the monthlies, pet? Would you like an aspirin?

I kept looking down the aisle for the orange-and-black coat. I tried to sleep. Each time a train rushed past on the other tracks the explosion of sound was terrifying. A winter moon had been abandoned in the daylight.

Naomi was waiting at the station for me. I carried my bag down the platform as if there was no injury, no missing piece. I followed her quietly round the supermarket. I wanted to touch the back of her skirt. She asked what I would like for Christmas dinner, whether we should celebrate – neither of us liked the holiday.

Soup's fine.

OK, soup. I need to go to the bank, she said. *I'll just give you money as your present.*

In the car, looking straight ahead, I bit my lip and told her what had happened. There was snow on the hilltops that made them look taller, more important. Deep teal over the horizon as the paler blue drew north.

Right, she said, *yes. It was a baby.*

I didn't know.

I was glad for the lack of tears. I was twenty-one. I had done without a childhood. It seemed too late.

She kept driving, didn't pull over and hug me when I said I was afraid.

He won't come, she said. *He's a coward and you've beaten him.*

But the air felt sprung and I could not shake the feeling of dread.

He's not really gone. I don't think I can handle him.

Take the tablets, Naomi said. *Do what the doctors say, Edith.*

Every time the phone rang in the cottage, I flinched, held my breath until it became apparent she was talking to someone else. I knew she was wrong. Ali was no minor player in the theatre of women. There would be a reckoning.

○

The sound of the medevac helicopter regularly working along the western flight path of the city unsettled me most. By late spring the sky was loaded with casualties. There were reports of ambulances not arriving to call-outs, hospitals declaring red status. There's a tipping point, when disasters that are civilly met overtake. Airport closures, food shortages, queuing as if in a war. The serious business of domestic death behind closed curtains, in a bedroom dressed safely with rose wallpaper, on the department-store bed.

In poorer boroughs, along lines of ethnicity and poverty, the virus spread wildly, exposing the country's bias, its rotten structures. There were the first desperate acts and breakages – fights at food banks, burgled shops, town halls vandalised. Crimes were reported and the police failed to come. Lives fell below the line; women whose secondary salaries the government would not protect, care workers struggling without equipment. The atmosphere was tindered.

People flouted the rules and marched. Protests were broken up; there were fines, arrests. It did not stop the gatherings.

This was the most dangerous phase, we were told by the prime minister. On screen, she looked gaunter, greyer; within weeks some private cosmeticist had whitened her hair. It was getting into us, infiltrating the mind as well as infecting the body. Cooperation was needed. The hours of darkness would therefore be barred for all but emergency personnel and cornerstone workers. People would have to prove why they'd left their homes; they would be asked for National Insurance numbers, attestations written before departure. And the military would be redeployed, to help manage the situation. The realist: you'd predicted this.

First they let us be spoiled children, now we must be given a discipline.

The complacency and dissonance I'd felt seemed ridiculous. There were good locks on the exterior doors of Burntcoat – the equipment downstairs was expensive. I hadn't before been concerned about every window, the main gate, the sensors in the yard. The shadow of a cat walking along the wall.

We'd not really been going out – occasionally you checked the restaurant or I went for bread. The first night of curfew had a clear, beautiful edge. It had rained and there was a mineral smell to the air, the river flowed sensually. We took the canoe out. You sat behind me, and we floated downstream, harmless criminals – under the branches of willows, through the cold tunnels of bridges. Boats were moored and fastened and mould had begun to gather along the door seals. The streetlights exposed us briefly before we disappeared back into darkness. By a jetty, something small and fast slipped into the inky water. Further down on the far bank, in the industrial estate, a car was burning, its fire reflected across the river. There were silhouettes moving. We glided past, the buoyant slipperiness of the boat responding to the lightest touch as we steered away. You shipped the paddle, spanned my neck with a hand, then took my hair between your fingers and pulled me gently backwards against your chest. I could hear your thoughts.

We will do this together.

Do you remember? Is that even possible? The dark, burning river. The turning tide; everything loosening beneath tight forces. None of it was happening and it was all unstoppable. Closing the door when we got back, and promising each other we would be all right. All we had was love, its useless currency, its powerful denial.

I remember. Musk on your body. A petrol taste in my mouth from the car fire. You stood looking at my bared chest with the eye of a sniper, the erection obvious in its unhoused state. The wall behind pinned me like an accomplice. The meat of your thighs braced between mine and the thrusts were compact, tests of strength. A final blare of pleasure and you sank to the floor, as if capable of being up on hind legs only to rut. The wall let me go. I stepped forward, put a hand on your head, and began spilling what you'd put into me.

o

No generation expects its crisis, the hole that opens at the centre, dragging everything in. Madmen and mesmerists,

God's heralds, a lone predicting scientist: the prophets are ignored, lost, ridiculed until they prove true. No one could see into the government meetings or read the hasty minutes, the arguments. No one knew what was not being revealed – the true estimate, the loss and cost. Parliament was suspended, the cameras in chamber switched off. The country was busy falling apart, tending its sick, tallying what was left in the cupboard and mourning freedom. Town after town, cities north and south, and into the quiet villages it spread.

I'll say it again. It was – it is – perfect. Perfectly composed, star-like, and timed for the greatest chaos, for transmission across borders, replication, creating galaxies of itself. Perfectly operating in each victim – the patient incubation, methodical progression through the body, careful removal of the defensive sheath. It ascends, hellishly, erupting inside its host. A fever that becomes critical, so destructive the body might kill itself. The virus dies with the host or survives, retreating deep into the cells, lying dormant.

Wards were closed off behind disinfectant bays, but videos kept being posted, of delirious, liquefying patients, last words, hands held through plastic sheets. New morgues were built and immediately overwhelmed. Twenty thousand, fifty thousand, two hundred thousand, half a million. There were no funerals. The bodies were burnt.

Crematoriums and hospital incinerators ran every hour of the day. Government-issue urns stood in ranks, waiting for families to be given permission to collect them: white, plastic, unremarkable in exterior and content.

There was no manual for this death, or palliative care. People died alone, in corridors, in waiting areas. They died in their beds, with infected children in the next room. It robbed entire families. Like a fiend from legend it seemed to smoke through windows and keyholes, able, when its name was spoken, to materialise. It was in the drops of fluid, under friable skin, on the breath. It was in the water, on the counter, the letter, the gift of each kiss.

Soon everyone knew someone infected. Kendra sent me a message:

Nova here. Nick incredibly unwell. Stay safe.

I slept in your arms, sweated, turned restlessly. Summer had arrived early; the days were hot and clear. The dogwoods along the river opened their bracts and the towpath grass grew high. We began to wake suddenly for no reason, jolted by a conviction that one of us was sick. Or by the sudden howl of a siren on the road nearby. We were in hiding, but it was harder and harder to keep our world airtight. I was working in the mornings, not able to concentrate. A bone in the throat seemed inconsequential.

There was a sense of something implicit when I looked at the sculpture, meaning I hadn't yet found. Shun had talked about the material, and the present, as undetermined, as wood's future memory. I kept thinking, time feels wrong, everything leads to failure. What is missing?

We found we could live together, in some ways thrive. There was still food at the restaurant and I'd always kept reasonable stock in the flat – old habits from a remote childhood. Naomi's weekly shops had been almost sacred. On Saturdays she cleared the boot of the car. She spent at least an hour loading the trolley, calculating costs, asking me to check the yellow-label bin, which I would do as quickly as I could. In the cottage garden were potatoes, leeks, radishes; the apples on the tree were small and sour, but with enough sugar we could bake them. Meals were always planned. You were good at moderation too; the first years of repatriation had been very hard, you told me, with your mother finishing shirts, taking laundry and shifts in factories – an extended family to support.

Halit understands 'yok', that's what my father always said. We can't have.

Such things are put into a person early, like religion. Only a few months before, I'd watched you fillet an entire salmon in the restaurant, removing thin wafers of outer silver, picking off the last few scales like sequins on the tip of the knife. The blade clicking against the bone architecture. I wondered what it would be like, once we were released from confinement. What kind of couple would we be? Forged, I thought, and strong.

Only a few vendors were working in the market, chancing prosecution if they exceeded hours. Rostam had sourced dried goods instead of flowers: figs, dates, cans of fruit. Next to the stalls, down a narrow alley, was a small bakery. In the mornings it opened, quickly sold what had been made, then pulled the shutters. I would go early while you slept, collect a loaf and run back home, carrying it warm under my arm. There was a new way of moving in the city, fleet, covered.

When it became known the bakery was still operating, more people began to come. One morning I arrived thinking I'd be the first, but the queue was already halfway along the alley. I took my place at the end. The door was not yet open, the smell of yeast and dough drifted from the ovens. People were standing apart, silently, glancing up and checking each other, swaying and adjusting their position, like nervous cattle. The eyes above masks and scarves were tense, avoidant. I sent you a message – *Stay in bed, all OK, back soon.*

A few minutes later, a man arrived. He was tall, dressed like an academic in a sports jacket, a big soft cap, and round, heavy-framed glasses. His face was bare, except for the smoke of grey stubble. He went straight to the bakery doors, swore, and glanced along the queue, then made an appeal to the first customer:

My wife isn't well, I need to get home.

The woman shook her head, stepped back. He tutted and tried again, and the next person in line protested, told him to wait.

Everyone has a sob story, mate.

The man ground his heel as he pivoted away and walked down the alley along the queue. He passed me by, aggressively close. Under his breath he was counting, as if every person in line was offensive. After a few moments, I glanced back. He was standing in the middle of the alley, jutting out.

The shutters rattled up and the bakery door opened. The woman serving was taking payment from customers first, then bagging up the bread inside and bringing it out. One loaf per person. The queue moved forward and stopped. I could hear the man talking loudly on his phone.

Don't be stupid, I said no. No!

Then, to no one in particular, he called out.

How long is this supposed to take?

The alley was still dim, the sun not yet high enough to enter. There was the crackle of bad energy in the air.

We're all supposed to just take it, are we?

Heads half-turned and then turned back. No one said anything.

I heard the man walking forward, his soles scuffing. His elbow clipped my arm. He seemed to be leaving, but then he paused near the door again. A young Asian woman was at the head of the queue. She'd paid and was waiting for her order.

Jeen, he said. *That you? I didn't see you properly.*

She nodded, said something quietly, looked down. He tried to talk to her, maybe she'd been his student, but she was clearly embarrassed, her body recoiling. Weeks of isolation had taken their toll; people were angry and afraid, the social norms had disappeared. The bakery assistant came out with a bag.

Look, he said, *I'll give you twenty quid for it.*

The young woman took the bread.

No, I can't.

Come on, he insisted, *you can queue up again, surely. What else have you got to do?*

She made to leave but he raised an arm, blocked her way in the narrow alley. He took money out of his pocket.

Here's forty, then.

She shook her head.

I can't take it.

Money; with its dirt and germs.

Can you just leave her alone, someone in front of me called out. The man wove his head round.

Oh, fuck off, I know her, he spat. *We're friends. We all say no, don't we – no, no, no! Her country said no we haven't made this fucking bug for the rest of the world!*

The young woman flinched away, tried to walk round him, but he caught and held her shoulders. He pulled open the pocket of her coat, stuffed the money inside.

Don't, the woman said, shrugging under his hand. *Don't touch me, please.*

The queue was breaking apart. Another woman walked away down the alley and the bakery door shut. I could feel something coming. My heart was thudding and there was a cold trickling feeling from my spleen. I took several steps forward, then stopped.

Just give it to me, Jeen. I've paid you now.

The man lunged for the bread, missed. The young woman hunched over, mantling what she held. He tried again and they tussled pathetically.

Stop, she shouted, her voice rising. *Please stop!*

He was not being rough but had her held firm by the coat, authoritatively, as a parent would a naughty child. People were circling the pair, trying to reason with the man, preparing to intervene. I was close and I didn't think. I moved in, pushed him hard on the chest. He stepped backwards and released the woman's coat. I've imagined what I might have said since, should have said, perhaps, but at the time I said nothing. The man's face was contorted; he'd given himself permission in this ugly new world. I hit him. My fist landed with force, but my wrist wasn't stern behind it. The face was puttyish and soft, with the dull edge of teeth. I felt something inside my hand click. His head seemed not to move much but the hat came off and he staggered back. He made a noise, incredulous or accepting of damage. It took a moment for blood to arrive. His mouth was deeply split, and as he curled back his lips, like a horse's flehmen response, red pooled beside the gum and smeared across the enamel. He bent over and spat.

The alleyway was quiet, braced for whatever would come next. The young woman glanced at me and took her chance to leave. My forearm began filling with pain. I opened my fingers and a hot spike travelled up the tendon. The man was looking up at me, running scenarios.

Bidge, he managed to say.

I was dizzy and unharnessed – could feel myself stepping in again, not stopping until he was limp on the pavement. Bloody saliva spooled from his mouth. He spat again. I made myself walk down the alley and away.

I went quickly back to Burntcoat, holding my arm against my chest. I let myself in through the studio door and sat on the bench. I was winded and weak after the rush of adrenaline. A sound like the sea was inside my head. You must have heard me. After a few minutes you came downstairs.

Edith?

I couldn't speak and you looked at me quizzically.

Shall I go back up? Shall I go to the bed?

Your head was tilted, the smile uncertain.

I've hurt my hand, I said. *I can't move it.*

You noticed me nursing the wrist then, came and sat next to me on the bench.

How?

You put a hand on my back, cupped the elbow of my arm without touching the injury. You touched my cheek.

Are you shivering? You're cold.

Yes. It was a shock.

Can you bend it? Turn it over, let me see.

I moved the arm, rotated it to show the knuckles. They were already swollen and red, and the skin on the tall middle bone was raked off.

Amına koyayım. Edith. Did anyone try to hurt you?

No. It was me. I'm sorry. I don't have the bread.

You pulled me against your shoulder, kept me held.

Who did you hit?

I don't know, a man.

What?

He didn't hurt me.

Look at your hand! We should go to the hospital.

We can't. I think it's just sprained.

You wanted a description, asked several times how you could recognise him, where he might be. Your body was solid with frustration; I'd not seen you so agitated.

134

It should have been me.

I took your hand with my good one, and your fingers curled tightly through mine.

It's all right, Halit.

No. Tamam. This is enough.

o

On Christmas Eve, as Naomi and I were sitting by the fire, I heard the sound of a car driving over the moor. There was snow in the valley, beginning to bank in the ditches. I'd been taking the sedative and was starting to feel better. Naomi was crocheting, pulling the threads over, hooking them – purple and green, purple and green, the movement relaxing to watch.

The engine was unmistakable, its keen, guttural production.

That's him, I said.

Naomi kept crocheting.

Are you sure?

I went to the cottage window, saw headlights lifting into the dusk, disappearing, and reappearing over the next brow.

Yes.

The panic felt small and frail, not really mine, uselessly flitting around like a moth.

All right, she said.

135

She was calm; not calm, but Naomi. She put the yarn and the square of material away in her sewing bag and stood. She had on the old gown and her hair was unbound. She did not take a coat from the peg or rush to find boots.

You stay here.

She opened the drawer of the dresser, then slipped something into her pocket. She released the latch, opened the front door and closed it gently behind her. Like a coward, I ran upstairs, shut off the bedroom light and half-closed the curtains. I watched Ali's car round the last bend of the lane. Naomi stood in the patch of window light, waiting. Her feet were bare on the thick rime of frost. In front of her, the twilight landscape bled together. Only the gorse had true definition on the horizon.

The car pulled up outside the cottage. Even behind the bedroom window I could hear loud music playing on its stereo. Music to wind him up. Ali waited until the song finished before he switched off the engine and got out. He pulled on his jacket. I heard his voice, the familiar droll confidence.

Nice to see you, Naomi. Is your daughter here, by any chance?

Edith's gone out.

Her voice was toneless. I peered down. She looked ragged, wild-haired, like a vagrant. Ali laughed sarcastically at her.

Right, course she has. Don't suppose you can make me a cup of tea. It was a hell of a drive.

No, Alistair, I can't make you a cup of tea.

There was a short silence.

Oh, OK. Then how about a piss, Naomi. Can I piss in your toilet, because I've been six hours in the car and this isn't much of a welcome?

No.

There was another silence. Their breaths smoked in the half-dark. Naomi's hair rose off her shoulders in the breeze; her feet looked tortured on the ice.

You know I spent a night in the cells because of her. Getting called a wife-batterer. Getting a light shone in my eyes every hour and using a stinking bog covered in twenty men's shit. The least you can do is let me use your nice clean bathroom, Naomi.

Behind glass, behind the barbiturate, it was easy to apprehend him. His base technique, his game of provocation. He would raise the stakes until he got a reaction.

Naomi did not repeat herself. They stood facing each other in the excruciating winter quiet, until Ali broke and shook his head.

I know she's in there, you spastic cow. She's sent out her dippy bint of a mother to do her dirty work.

His voice was lower and sharper now; he'd been castled

and was furious. He cocked his head, looked at Naomi from a different angle. I couldn't see her full face but I knew its incapacity, the glass wall everything slid off. She was hard to abuse. She was neurally elliptical, would say only what she wanted to. She put her hand in the pocket of her gown. For a second I thought, it's a knife, she's about to kill him. It will be logical, practical, like cutting butter to spread on toast. But she withdrew a stack of folded money, her Christmas gift to me. She held it up, not away from her body but close to her breast.

What, he said, *some kind of bribe? Are you buying your daughter back?*

No. It's petrol money.

Ali shook his head and glared at her.

Naomi. It's Christmas fucking Eve. Where do you think I'm going to go now?

She remained poised, the money offered like feed to a resistant animal that would eventually come. Her gown was terrible-looking, its velvet coarsened and worn, almost mythical. Ali's coat was made of sable panels, the orange hazard on the back redundant.

I should have gone down, intervened, put a stop to it, but I didn't. Ali must have known I was there, watching, but he didn't call out. He wanted a fight, and Naomi was enough for his purpose, better in some ways, a new partner – one he suspected of both weakness and potential he couldn't measure. All the times he'd tested her, trying to find the angles, spark the kindling, but she was retardant.

Ali unzipped his fly, took out his cock and let go an arc of piss that steamed in the cold air. It splattered on the ground around Naomi's feet, hit the hem of her robe. He held the soft fat shaft with one hand, proudly out from his body. She did not flinch or step back. When he was done, he reached and took the money. They blurred together for a moment, their voices inaudible, like conspirators. It was too awful. I turned to put on a jumper and made my way downstairs. I pulled on my boots and unlatched the front door. The Escort was leaving; the engine gunned as Ali reversed round, its tail lights two red eyes drawing back over the moor. I don't know if he saw me.

After a moment, Naomi came inside. There was no injury but her face was pale, with two garish marks of colour in her cheeks. She smelled of cold air and, faintly, the wheaty odour of urine. I wanted to hug her but she was already moving past into the bathroom. I heard the rattle of the plug chain and water running in the sink, the tap squealing shut. Beyond the front door, the white ground had been turned over and stained yellow, a wild patch where some form of contest and defeat had occurred. I shut and latched the door. There didn't seem to be a real threat any more.

When Naomi came out of the bathroom she was still wearing the gown, and it was dripping from the bottom. It was hard to look at her.

Are you all right?

Yes, she said. *Are you hungry?*

Not really.

I am.

We sat at the kitchen table, with bowls in front of us. Naomi lowered her spoon into the soup, lifted and sipped. There was the faintest tremor to the silver oval, to the hand holding it.

I forgot to put in salt again, she said.

No, it's nice. It's good.

I tried to eat. The bread pulped and reformed in my mouth and I couldn't swallow. I felt my face collapsing and the first spasms hit.

Naomi looked up at the sound.

What is it? she said. *Does your tummy still hurt?*

My forehead bloomed with pain. I clenched my eyes shut and felt my fingers digging into the piece of bread, balling it tight.

Edith? Edith.

The spoon clinked in Naomi's bowl. She took the roll gently out of my hand and held my wrist. Her response was automatic.

He could have hurt you. You could have died.

Something surged against my chest, rose through me uncontrollably, fighting to get out. My body shook. I couldn't stop the noise, the stream of tears. I was eight, it was Christmas; she hadn't collapsed in the street, she was smiling, her eyes quick and expressive as I showed her the doll's house in the toyshop.

No, she said. *He was just angry you left him. I told him the hotel at Scotch Corner would be open. Would you like something else to eat?*

I shook my head, mucus streaming from my nose and mouth.

When I calmed, she lifted her hand away. She picked up my bowl and emptied the soup back into the pan, lit the flames underneath to reheat it.

o

After the incident, you wanted to empty the storeroom at the restaurant. There was fish in the freezer, which would soon expire, and bulk-sized dried goods. There were now more reports of looting and violence, chaos at hospitals. In the city, two armed men had been shot by soldiers near a food bank. The virus was still transmitting. Kendra's messages had stopped – she was sick too. It would be better to make a final trip, you said, and withdraw completely.

We talked about giving supplies away.
What do you think?
Maybe. No, fuck them.
Another value system had arrived. You were angry, trusted neither the people nor the leaders – a familiar depressing feeling. Some calculation was being made by the government, about the number of infections, the breaking of the wave. Until then, we would have to endure.

My wrist was bandaged in crêpe; you'd wrapped it very neatly, to my surprise. The military service, you explained, when there was little to do but patrol the border, watching for feudal village activity, learning to polish, drill, practising first aid.
And watching pornography.
With the confession, you glanced up from doctoring my wrist.
Sorry.
Why? I don't care. I'd have watched it too, I'm sure. What kind did you watch?
You laughed, looping the white roll over and under. There was a dull ache in the joint and the occasional throb of pain travelled up my arm. The whole area felt stiff.
Come on, distract me, please.

Well, I had to take it off the men, usually – what's the word?

Confiscate.

Yes, confiscate.

What was your rank?

Captain.

Oh, Captain.

You gave a heavy sigh.

Everyone has to do it. Not everyone, actually – Hassan, who I worked with before the restaurant, didn't. He was considered European. Is it too tight?

No, it feels OK. So, what did you watch?

You shook your head, trying not to smile.

What did you like?

I don't know.

You do!

Well, all kinds. When the woman is in charge.

Oh.

We can't talk about this.

I leaned forward and kissed you on the neck, very softly, brushed my mouth up towards your ear, a zone you couldn't resist.

Tell me, I whispered.

You sighed again, capitulating or deciding to play along.

When you can see it going into her mouth, and everything she is doing with her tongue.

Do you like it a long way into her mouth? Deep?

143

A red patch was beginning to form on your neck.

No, over the end, licking it.

What else?

When she is on top, she really wants it, and the camera can see her ass lifting up and down and it . . .

I finished your sentence.

When you can see her riding on the dick and the dick is really wet and getting worked.

Oh my God! Definitely!

You laughed again, shocked by the frankness, and caught between discomfort and pleasure. You kept looping the band of crêpe, maintaining its neat rows.

Do you like it when she is shaved?

Not really, that doesn't remind me of anything.

It's better if it's real?

Of course.

Some men just like to watch – they prefer it.

No. How can that be better?

I guess they like to see a woman getting fucked.

I always wanted to fuck her. I don't think I can finish this properly if the conversation keeps going.

I waited for you to tie the bandage, splitting apart and tucking the crêpe. The pinch of jealousy, as your courteous, discreet front spoiled and experience spilled out, was both painful and exciting. Shadowy scenes from your past, and I was a voyeur. You were kneeling beside me, had been looking down throughout the explicit interview. Now you held my gaze. Your eyes were brightly minted, full of mischief, mild disgrace, the glimmer of arousal.

Why are we talking about this?

It's a painkiller.

I lifted my arm. The dressing ran in neat chevrons to my finger joints, shortening the digits to stumps. You shook your head.

Some of it was very bad. What they were doing to the women in the films, I mean. I don't like those things.

Some people do.

I don't. Actually I don't know if it was a film or a crime where someone made a video.

The line in the centre of your brow deepened. I knew you enough now; there were two sides close together, different states – from levity, the blue of an iris quickly cooled, becoming glacial, aloof.

It's hard, being away from your family. No friends, no lover. Even for only a year. I had to talk to soldiers who were going crazy. I don't want to say it but it has to come out somewhere. There were guns and men. A film is better.

We could talk about most things. But there were native compartments full of history I couldn't access, and in which I would never belong.

Did you have to use a gun?

You mean did I kill anyone? I saw someone get shot. The border runs through such old villages, people have been there hundreds of years. The same families – it's tribal. A man crossed over to see his fiancée. The watchtower caught him. We had to take the body back and explain. So, I was responsible, yes.

You were on your knees, upright, with your hands on your hips. A man rearing up from prayer, or refusing to bow, his chest exposed to everything incoming. I wasn't sure what to say.

So stupid, he was just running. That could have started something.

It was hard to reconcile – the genial partner with hair now falling below the shoulder, and the soldier packing the corpse, your translator doing his best to relay an apology and keep control in a settlement stoked with grief; you turning and walking away with rifle crosshairs on your back. Your smile was tight, not a smile but a defence. He will be better at this than me, I thought. We will be safe.

After a week I was using the hand gently. It wasn't broken – I was sure I could drive and even help lift food into the van. I wanted to come to the restaurant but you refused.

You have to let it heal. You've got to be able to use it to work.

Are you sure?

Yes, I can carry the things.

Maybe you should take your residency papers.
Do you think I need that?
They are stopping people.
I've been here ten years!
I don't think it makes a difference now.

You emptied the last few items out of your rucksack, checked your pockets for a mask, your ID. We stood by the door, preparing, as if it were an airlock, with protean space beyond.

Will you cover up? And wear the gloves?
Yes. I'll be quick. It's fine.
OK, bye. I kissed you.
Bye, canım.

An hour later you arrived back. I heard you walking up the iron staircase, slowly, pausing between each step – weighed down with supplies, I thought. I went out onto the fire escape to help you. You were clutching the rails, looking down, stepping upwards slowly, lifting only one leg, then bringing the other beside it. You had no bag and your shirt was hanging loose. On the street was a military Land Rover, its window open, the driver waiting and watching.

Halit. Are you all right?
You didn't look up; you were concentrating on the stairs.
You weren't arrested, were you?

You raised your face. There was bruising round an eye and the temple was misshapen, egging out.

Oh shit. What happened?

I moved to help but you lifted a hand and winced.

Go back in.

When you got to the top of the stairs the Land Rover pulled away. There was a grinning cut under your eye. It was not until you were through the door and I saw your back that I realised the extent of it. The shirt was torn and bloody, and underneath, wet red gashes.

Oh God.

You bent forward, trying to remove your shoes, but stalled and gave a sharp cry.

Please take them, you said.

I crouched and undid the laces. You heeled the shoes off.

Why did the army pick you up? Did they do this?

The cheek was swelling madly under your eye.

No. They drove me to a clinic but it was full. One of the guys pulled out some glass but I need to wash the rest.

In the bathroom I helped you undress. You managed the buttons but shouldering out of the shirt was impossible. I gently lifted the material off your back and peeled the sleeves down your arms. There were eight or nine serious lacerations, surrounded by raw grazes and crusts of grass. The cuts were not bleeding heavily; one or two looked deep, gaping through the inner layers. A long shard was still embedded.

Hang on.

I ran to get a stool and you sat, lowering yourself rigidly.

Did they give you anything?

Aspirin.

Aspirin? That's it?

I didn't take it – I'm allergic.

What? I didn't know that.

It's fine.

It's not fine. Where are the bloody police? People are just attacking anyone?

I took the tweezers from the cabinet, tried to clasp the hilt of the glass shard but the metal hands slipped off as I pulled. You made a bitten-in noise, flinched.

Sorry, I'm sorry.

I put my hand on your shoulder, tried again less tentatively, and the shard came out, a long transparent needle. A trickle of blood ran from the puncture, dripped off your back onto the floor.

I really think you need some stitches, Halit.

You stood slowly.

The water will take the rest out.

You stood with your hands on your hips, breathing hard. I switched on the shower.

Can you make it hot?

It's going to sting.

I turned the setting, and steam began to plume from the cold surface of the bath. You undid your belt, pushed down the jeans and shorts. I bent to help pull them off your ankles and take off your socks. There were marks on your thighs and calves, crescents, the first bloom of bruises.

Do you want to tell me what happened?

I just want to get clean.

OK, let me help you.

I need the toilet.

Shall I leave?

It doesn't matter.

I stood aside, turned my head and heard the trickle into the bowl, a grunt of discomfort as you lowered the lid. You stepped into the bath, gasped as the water ran onto your chest. Your back was demonic, hatched with holes and stroked by lines of blood. You looked like a creature whose spines had been pulled out. The last, freshest socket was still weeping red. For a minute, you let the water drill your front, your face. Then with huge effort of will you turned and put your back under the spray, crying out as if receiving the injury all over again. You tried to withstand it, but the wails were involuntary and awful, lamb-like. Water ran pinkly round your feet. Your face was distorted underneath its flow; the expression altered so the pain looked ecstatic.

After, you sat, stunned, flushed with heat and trembling, waiting for the air to dry you. You told me what had happened. They'd seen you go into the restaurant. They'd been very quick, so were probably used to doing it by now. You'd locked the door behind, but they smashed and came through the window, took produce, the little money there was in the float. One of them kicking and stamping on your legs so you wouldn't follow.

As if I would really have tried to stop them, you said hollowly.

I dressed the cuts, stuck cotton pads and tape over the worst. You tried to put on a T-shirt but it was too uncomfortable, so you sat next to the stove, upright and immobilised, then exhausted from the posture, leaning on a pile of cushions, the cotton patches staining. I found some old tobacco and hash, rolled a cigarette and we smoked. Neither of us said what we were thinking – that you'd been badly exposed.

That night you slept on your stomach. Every time you began to move onto your side the pain disturbed us.

Are you OK?

I'm so stiff.

I took your hand, stroked the places that did not hurt.

Halit?

Your eye was open. Then it closed. For weeks you'd reached for me across the bed, in the layer between awareness and unconsciousness, bonding warmly to my hip and waist. Now I guarded the space between my front and your injuries. I adjusted the sheets, as if you were a child. You were awake or unconscious, unreachable either way.

That was the last time you went out. The days after were sober and quiet. You slept a lot, moved carefully from the bed to the chairs, or out into the yard to feel the sun. There were heavy purifying rains, then sunshine again – the plant pots were growing wildly, new flowers had seeded themselves in the patches of earth, the gaps in the wall. You kept going to the sink and drinking water. My birthday passed; I made a small meal, and we sat and ate quietly, and it was enough. But a feeling of violation remained.

We cleaned the cuts every other day. They began to heal, bonding blackly, and could be flexed without reopening; occasionally a bolt of pain jolted you. I found myself inadequate, didn't really know how to cheer you, what to say. The restaurant was ruined, you were certain; even after repair, how would it withstand the economic collapse that was sure to come? I kissed your cheek.

I'm sorry. I know how hard you worked.

The gentle sex, on our sides, only brought momentary escape. You drew the blanket up, hid us. We were back to being polite and cautious.

Do you want toast?

No, thanks.

You didn't eat today.

OK, then.

Are you going to work in the studio?

No.

Please don't let me being here interfere.

For something to do, I cut your hair at the kitchen table. The dark drifts slipped to the floor. The first few greys were appearing above your forehead and in the middle of your beard.

Hold still.

The scissor blades worked crisply; you didn't move. I tipped your head: the neck tautened, offering an artery, and the harsh whiskers above your lip sprinkled downwards.

What a shame. You looked like Jesus.

That would not go down well with my family.

Jesus was sexy.

Not as sexy as Muhammad.

By the way, I have clippers if you want.

What? Shave it all off? Why do you have them?

I scrolled back in my phone and showed you a photograph of the award ceremony, my stripped scalp, the tattoo. You looked at the picture.

This is you.

Yes.

You look – really thin. And strange.

Yeah, I know.

I mean, you look very different. How do I not know about that! Where is it . . . ?

You pulled me down, sat me on your knee and parted sections of the hair above my ear until you saw the ink.

What is it?

It's my mother's name, written in Kanji.

You turned my head and held my face in your hands. You kissed me with a new, uncovered mouth, the old mouth from our beginning, when we'd stood in the winter street.

Don't look sad, I said, *it was just a difficult time.*

Worse than now?

In some ways.

Edith, you whispered, *you are my love. And I am quite afraid of you.*

I liked it. Part of me enjoyed the crisis, I admit. There was relief, almost, in the promised worst, and I think that being two, as we were, so dependent on each other and against the world, was like my upbringing. Artists don't age, no matter how serious the game they play, how fine and cunning their creations. Even now, can I say what's real?

This bed.

The sky, in the window, and all its unsettled colours.

This condition, so weak, so unsexual and defenceless, a state of being that has almost passed but still is.

The black, flickering door.
You.

I'm still a halfling on the moors, finding berries, cupping from the underground river, making things out of twigs and thorns. The world exists through recreation, how it is perceived. You were a tear in all that, a gift of sudden truth. Because of you I could say, with certainty, I believe in it, all.

o

At the table you lifted your arm and reached for the salt, and I saw the rash around the point of bone. Wet, yellowish, with a red halo. There were small bubbles under the skin with pale liquid inside. I caught your arm and held it. Some blisters had burst and their pus was already crusting.

What?

You tried to see, twisting your arm round, then went to the bathroom mirror and held up the elbow. Under your breath, you said a word I didn't recognise, then closed your eyes, and your head fell back. I felt the first sick rising of alarm.

Did you burn it? Or anything.

Silence.

Halit?

No.

We'd both been counting the days – nine since you'd come back hurt.

You faced the ceiling, blind, like the head of a plant waiting for light's instruction. I tried to find something to say. Then your attention snapped back, you opened your eyes and looked at me.

Do you have anything?

No, I don't think so.

We have to check.

We stood apart in the bathroom and undressed. There was no thrill; even when you'd been hurt and I'd taken down your shorts I'd noted, for a fraction of a second, the bones of your hips, the brownish penis in a nest of dark hair.

My skin was clear. You made me turn several times, looking everywhere, in my armpits, the backs of my knees. The examination was horribly thorough.

I'm fine. Please stop.

No, turn again. Lift up your feet.

Perhaps you were delaying.

Halit, let me look at you properly. Please.

You stood still as a pillar and I walked round, squatted. There were more marks on your lower back, in the ridge between buttocks. They looked like infant sores, fever blisters, nothing I'd seen in adulthood even when travelling.

Do you think it's nova?

Your voice was small, urgent.

Yes.

I tried to hug you but you held my shoulders and stood me away.

No, come on, you can't do that!

You walked out of the bathroom into the bedroom and began stripping the sheets.

We have to wash everything. I've touched everything!

Halit, stop, please.

You pulled the covers off the pillows, half frantic, half furious, full of self-reproach.

I will clean here. Then I will go back to my flat. I'm a fucking idiot.

You bundled the sheets, held them between your fists, every muscle in your torso stark. Violence or flight; I didn't know you in this state, didn't know which might happen. Your face was concentrated, stony, the bruises on your temple faded to pale grey. No small dispute can prepare for the first real conflict, its size and sere.

In another version you took up your clothes, dressed, and left, slamming the door. I did not see you again. It hangs there, the possibility, in which we are cut apart and freed and lost from each other. In that version, emptiness reaches the edge of the frame; nothing populates it. Everything is the colour of clay. My whole life is lived differently, or is not lived. But you were incapable of abandonment, of refusing kindness.

Stop. I have it already, I said. *If you do, I do.*

You shook your head and looked away.

No, you don't.

Yes.

I walked forward and took the sheets, and you let go hesitantly, as if putting a small child into the sea. I dropped them and placed my hand on your chest. You kept shaking your head, denying everything, my touch, your acquittal, the disease.

You can't leave. Please don't leave.

Then we were in each other's arms.

We were healthy, with no other conditions. We were young, strong. We would be OK. The assurance we gave each other after we'd stepped from the embrace was as fervent as it was false.

Later, you called the medical phone line. There was a substantial wait, almost an hour, during which you listened to a recorded message with information about the virus, and Sibelius repeating. You paced the room, stopping in front of Jonah's photographs, those black-and-white moments from an incidental age.

The calcifying music suddenly stopped and an advisor took your name and details, asked what symptoms you had. She asked you to take your temperature. There was no fever. Your pulse seemed normal. You answered a series of questions.

No, no, yes there's someone with me, no they are not ill.

She recited standard information, the stages of the disease, its progressive indications – nothing we didn't know. You were like a schoolboy, listening so hard, making notes. A couple of times you asked the woman to repeat what she'd said. At the end of the call she gave you another phone number; you glanced up at me, then circled and underlined it twice.

We sat together at the table. You made coffee. Next to the cups I put small glasses of vodka. Now we were truly a couple. Everything before seemed like an introduction, a first dance. You rubbed the back of your head, where the hair was shorter and sharp.

Was she even a medic? I asked.

I don't think so.

What else did she say?

Just the same things. Drink a lot. They don't want you to go to hospital.

She said that?

Not in those words.

But if we need to go . . .

I could already sense my failure, a feeling of being mired in old duties, with no experience. We did not talk about the odds, or the research, though we'd both been checking our phones, every new article. You caught my eye, smiled tightly.

So, I'll just get better, then I'll look after you if we need to. Deal?

Deal.

There's no good way to wait for disaster. Redundancy, a hurricane, surgery – the days, the hours before are already afflicted, emptied of true productivity and slippery with fear. I saw you looking at the rashes in the mirror, as if reminding yourself. A low headache began, particular, you said, intimate, like a migraine, and body heaviness like a precursor to a cold, nothing extreme. It was possible to believe the onset would be manageable. There were people – a few – who'd suffered mildly, said it was no worse than flu.

The next morning you could not drink coffee. You pushed the cup aside.

I'm sorry, I don't want it.

Do you need more sleep?

It's not that. The taste. Wow, first it kills your nationality.

You smiled wanly at your joke. I nodded, but a strange predictive guilt had left me feeling withdrawn. I went down into the studio and sat doing nothing, itching in the hot light of the windows. The wolf and crane were still unfinished, their positioning obviously wrong. Timbers were stacked on pallets, leaning in architraves, and the lump of multi-armed driftwood we had hauled back from the beach seemed nothing more than tidal wrack, a sea folly. Worse – it looked viral. The discomfort of not working, of false progress, was almost equal to the pressure outside the studio. What was the point of any of it? Finally, everything would rot and collapse. This piece, anything I made, would become meaningless, unknowable as a prehistoric spiral on stone.

As I came back upstairs, I could hear you talking on the phone, fast, formally and affectionately, to your parents. The few phrases I could understand were lost in the flow.

Baba, evet, evet.

When you hung up you looked relieved.

My family.

Are they OK?

My sister was sick, but she's getting better.

That's really good.

Yes.

For the first time you sounded hopeful, cautiously so. I wasn't sure if they knew you were here, what privacies and secrets you had kept.

Did you tell them you might be . . . unwell?

No. There's nothing they can do. My mother would worry herself to death.

We were still impelled towards each other – a different sickness. Your body responded to mine, to its exposed skin. The nights were hot. We lay close, without covers, the window open, a semen-scented pollen drifting in.

I feel like I've known you a long time.

It is. It's been a lot of time.

You couldn't help looking, at my chest, the warm, flat nipples, pale-blue veins snaking under their surface, the dark badge. You were hesitant, tired, but the driver was the same, hardening, and wouldn't lie down. You couldn't hide it. I reached to touch. I didn't know any better comfort.

You groaned, when I wrapped my hand round, began to move it. I stroked a thumb across the secreting tip, circling the skin's arrowhead. You responded but were tense, conflicted.

Do you think it's OK?

I don't know. Why not? Yes.

I brought my head down, started with immense care and softness, my mouth like some wet, fragile creature alighting. I wanted you to forget, tried to take you away.

You had begun touching me, trying to reciprocate, but the receipt was too exquisite; you gave up and lay back against the pillow. You brought your hand to your face. I would have kept going until climax, which seemed not far away, but you roused abruptly, turned me onto my back, knelt between my legs and fitted yourself. You began to move. Your hands were either side of my head, your hips bucking against my thighs, determined, the buttocks squeezing, forcing the energy forward. It seemed perfect, a perfect escape, and then after a few moments it seemed wrong, and unnatural. Something about the position, or the mood, failed. The interior was less sensual, less active, walls of meat. You began moving faster, indisputably, freighted by the sense it wasn't working. The fuck became a commitment.

I was mute, and couldn't tilt to an angle where anything felt right. There was a different smell to your body, in the glands, coppery, sour. It's the sickness, I thought, altering his chemistry. I found my eyes full of tears and I arched, trying to hide the emotion with arousal, a pretence, but you sensed it, heard the strained note in my voice, saw dark, wet spots on the cotton pillowcase. You stopped, felt my cheek with a thumb and looked down at me, the flesh of your face collapsing forwards. There was unusual sweat on your brow.

What is it?
Nothing.
I'm sorry.

163

I put my hand on your hip, pressed the fingers into the flesh.

Don't stop, it's fine.

It's not fine.

You withdrew, sat back. Your chest was glazed too, and you were struggling for air. You looked ill.

It was the first time we had abandoned anything. A broken arrangement, and now I was sure everything else could break. I desperately wanted to take us back again and leant forward, tried to encourage the hardness back. I tasted myself on you, the rivery flavour. You put your hand on my head, but the feeling had gone. It softened and shrank in my mouth. You apologised again. I hated myself in that moment, the failure of seduction, being stripped of love's means. I got up from the bed as if we'd argued, and left the bedroom. I heard you calling after me.

Through the window were the dark roofs of the city, stars that multiplied every night as the pollution cleared, so many they became their own bright solution. A moon, cut away by fractions, always growing back. Everything was a number. The days in confinement. The hours until true sickness arrived. The percentage of survivors. Degrees of lethal hyperthermia. I thought I knew the lessons of impermanence and resilience. Naomi's. Shun's.

I think I know them now, yet find no solace. Is it possible to work with a material so long and still not understand its condition? We are figures briefly drawn in space; given temporary form in exchange for consciousness, sense, a chance. We are ready-mades, disposables. How do we live every last moment as this – savant dust?

You crossed the length of Burntcoat silently, on the feet of a predator, a ghost. The lamp went on. The living space filled with dim objects and shadows. I felt you standing behind me, your arms circling my stomach and breasts. The hold was tight, uncomfortable, not enough to keep us together were we to fall. I couldn't see your face, only imagine who you might be.

The door of the bathroom was open. Opposite, in the long mirror, a woman was being held out of the darkness. Her breasts were pinned and distorted, the nipples like amblyopic eyes. Her thighs shone pale and obvious, the pubic hair twisted into a damp curl as if she'd recently had intercourse. Her arms lay prone at her sides. Whoever had claimed her could see her as she viewed herself, fully exposed, like a woman on offer in a window, or marble statue in the esplanade. A ritted hole in her stomach where she had been made.

This is not the story. This has never been the story.

The woman was still, and then her hands reached up and back into the darkness, her pelvis tipped towards the alignment of desire. She stirred whatever was behind her, woke it to perform. Its hands moved to cup her breasts, their significant weight and shape, their erect centres. She stepped her legs apart, commanded attention. The hand went to it, two fingers working the slippery seam, burying into the passageway, bringing moisture to the hood. She watched the pleasure, liked what she saw, her own intoxication.

She bent forward, and a lover was partially revealed, dressed in shadows, unidentified. She pushed back, found the fix. Her hips were held. She was jolted forward, once, twice, again and again filled and emptied and filled. Her flesh shook and her breasts swung. She looked up through a veil of hair as the darkness slapped against her.

The woman in the mirror watched me too. My lover's head was tipping back, exactly the same – its mouth a dark orifice – then falling forward, and righting. We watched each other, copied each other, patrons of the same club. When one of us screamed, the noise that came from the twin's mouth was primal and victorious. Behind us, released from burden, our partners spilled hotly over our backs, jerking the last of it out with gripped hands.

o

I couldn't sleep that night. I sat beside you in bed and stroked your hair. I was sore and wired and had passed the point of any comfort. You'd made tea from the sage in the yard, the soft green ears torn up and sinking in the mugs, as you used to make from the plants on the hillside near Yeniköy. Your mother's cure, a remedy for all sick and aggravated states. The taste was earthy, almost perspirant. You'd taken a few sips then lain down, and were sleeping curled on your side. You looked pale in the dawn light, the sheets rumpled around you. An oyster in its shell. The cuts on your back were dry and sealed.

Even before symptoms truly arrived, there seemed to be profound change, in the way you moved, or sat – against the wall, staring down, your eyes dumbly asking for something that couldn't be given. The process of illness is also the dissolution of the self. This time there was no instant switch, no click of the fingers as the brain spat its mess. Instead, a week of increasing debility. Your breathing became more difficult, took extra energy, even at rest. It was as if your cavities had been filled with stone aggregate, the way Sean ballasted interior structures. You were so heavy. I helped you between rooms; you had to sit halfway, like an old man. We knew about the cerebral effect – a strange fog, an inability to concentrate.

At worst, it was like encephalitis. You rambled, wanted to tell me things, about your family, about hitchhiking in the south, but the stories were muddled, the point of interest was forgotten.

He is my oldest friend – but I don't remember his name.
What is his name?
Cem?
Cem!

It was nearing midsummer. I was wearing shorts and a vest, but even under several covers you were wracked by chills. I lit the stove. It made no difference. The aches seemed intolerable, marrow-deep, and your spine was a belt of nerves conveying discomfort throughout your body. You'd told me about the illnesses you'd had as a child – asthma, the collapsing lung, giardiasis – this was like nothing else. I'd seen frightening things, my mother's stapled skull; I thought, I can tend to him, manage, it will be a form of intimacy. We had accelerated through a lifetime's relationship and now there would be the carer's duty.

When you were too weak to get up I helped you piss into a container, emptied it. I brought you small dishes, mashed fruit, broth, things I thought you could tolerate. You were nauseous, couldn't eat, and didn't want water.

You've got to drink. Remember what she told us.

But you groaned and rolled away; lay your head back down like a slab against the pillow.

The odour of an unwashed body, of disease – that same tang I'd first smelled, but gathering, ripening. You'd always taken such care, washing. I began to hate the sound of my own voice, its unreplied repetitions.

Here's some water. I've brought you fresh water. Would you like water?

Your lips were drying and flaking and the weight was falling off. I began to panic, used more force, hauling you up against the bedstead.

OK, come on, we're going to try to get something in.

I left you there, listing to the side, and went to fetch a glass of orange juice. You lifted a hand when I brought it close, weakly fending it away.

Halit, you have to. Please. Try.

There was a minute of childish opposition, a tightly closed mouth, distressed sounds. Then you relented, took the glass, spilling it as you lifted it to your mouth and drank half, forcing it down your throat.

OK, that's really good.

You sat still, breathing erratically, and after a few seconds retched. You pushed me away and vomited over the bed, a lurid orange mess, more than could possibly have gone into your stomach. The violence of your body's rejection gave you some strength. You staggered up and made it to the bathroom, closing the door halfway behind you. I could hear what was happening, the water in the bowl splattering every few seconds, then hollow sounds.

When it seemed the bout had passed, I knocked on the door and pushed it open. You were on your knees, gripping the toilet, your body shaking. I could see every rib. You made an attempt to get up, failed and slumped to the side. I came to you, put a hand on your back. You were shivering and sweating. There was a rotten silage smell. I wasn't sure what to do. I ran to the cupboard and got a blanket, covered you.

Are you OK?

The question was stupid.

I have to sort out the bed. I'll be as fast as I can. OK? OK? I'll be back in a minute.

I left you quaking on the floor, went out and balled up the bedding. The smell of the vomit made me gag; it contained something noxious. I stripped off the layers; everything had soaked down. Quickly I sponged the mattress, towelled it, put on a new sheet. There was a bucket in the studio with hardened resin inside; I left it by the bed and went back to the bathroom.

Beside your head on the tiles was a small colourless patch of vomit, umbilical saliva attaching it to your mouth. And another smell, manure-like, faecal. There was a soiled patch on the back of your shorts. You looked unconscious, despite the whimpers at the end of each breath. A streak of reddish vomit was on the cistern where you'd tried to reach for the flush.

I stood staring down, as if at a destitute in the street or an animal destroyed on the road. Just go to him, I told myself. I crouched down, lifted your head a fraction. Your eyes opened, lost focus, closed again. I knew I should be acting like a softer authority, crooning words, reassuring you. I moved the blanket. Sweat was rolling from under your arms and down your chest, collecting on the tiles.

Halit. Can you wake up? Halit!

Your eyes opened, swam, then focused.

Uyuyor muydum?

It's Edith.

Was I sleeping?

Your voice was hoarse, burnt by the expulsions.

You passed out. We have to wash you. We have to get you cleaned.

Somehow we moved, crawling and lumbering to the bath, and I hauled you in. Your skin was hot. Your beard matted.

Lift. Lift up.

You looked confused, hadn't realised your condition.

I need to take these things off.

You raised your backside, and I wrangled the clothing, trying not to look at the contents. It was vile. I turned my head, reared back. The humiliation was too much; your face began to fold and you started crying.

I'm sorry, you whispered. *I can do it myself.*

No, don't, it's OK. Honey, it's OK.

I lifted the head of the shower down and turned it on.

Can you hold this?

You fumbled and held it loosely while I took the underwear to the kitchen, bagged it in plastic and put it in the bin. My head was full of static, like electrical rain, there were thousands of tiny shocks inside. I washed my hands and returned to you. I tried to heft your weight, soaped, gently rinsed the gullies. Twice more your bowels opened, and I washed the liquid down towards the drain, started the process of washing you again. There was a brutality to the procedure; I was inept, clumsy, you didn't mean to fight but your efforts to help felt like resistance. I ignored the indignity, tried to talk about other things, then operated in silence. It seemed to take hours, though it must only have been ten or twenty minutes. Finally, some stage passed; you seemed emptied and meeker. I dried you, wrapped you in a blanket, supported you back to bed. The bone of your hip was like a blade in my side.

This was the labour required. It can't get worse or more dehumanising, I thought. He will do it for me too, and there will be nothing left hidden between us.

Your temperature was rising towards forty. I opened the apartment windows, brought a fan next to the bed. I was desperate to get liquid into you, any way that would not shock your body. I heated a pan of water to room temperature and spooned it into your mouth, one spoon every minute. It seemed to work. Then you gestured for the bucket. If I had had children I might have known better, not been so complacent. I would have put towels on the bed, not new sheets. I learnt the hard way, as parents do, as the nurse in triage does. I rolled you to the side of the bed, took away dirty linen, replaced it. I sponged you clean, put padding between your legs. The fluids became water-based, dregs.

When your temperature ran over forty I called the emergency number, waited for an operator.

He has novavirus. He needs help. I can't look after him properly.

I sounded pitiful. The voice on the other end was calm, normal. There were no intensive-care beds available, no ward beds, no clinics, what I was doing was correct, the fever had to mount and run its course naturally. If a seizure occurred, I should protect the neck, teeth, tongue and soft tissue in the mouth. I didn't understand what she was saying.

He needs to go to hospital. He's incredibly unwell. I'm not a doctor!

Please stay calm. We advise you not to move him.

I wanted to scream at the woman.

You aren't here, you can't see him.

I let you down. I know I did. I was scared. Your body was on fire. Red patches formed deep in your skin – the olive tone was gone and you became nationless, just a creature, white and stemless on the bed. Insensate. There was nothing I could do but watch you burn, listen to you mumbling and shouting out. I washed the sheets and hung them in the yard, indelible stains left in the fibres. I brought up a piece of tarpaulin from the studio, placed it under you, a shameful waterproof mat. With every movement it clicked and rustled. I wanted so badly to sleep, just for an hour, but the adrenaline was effervescent in my body, the subconscious images were invasive and awful. I was incinerating your carcass, holding the blowtorch to your rotting face. Something was moving inside you, black and oily inside the cocoon.

I couldn't leave you for more than a few minutes, to eat, wash my hands, use the bathroom. I knew I couldn't cope. I saw myself walking through the door, out onto the street. I saw myself walking to the edge of the city, into the fields, down the straight, unerring Roman road, all the way to the lowlands and into the sheltering granite of the mountains. The vision was so clear, so right; it was the easiest of all choices. The choice my father had made.

The choice of ancestors crossing the ice, abandonment of burden, leaving behind the limiting needful thing. I rationalised it insanely. Who knew you were here? Not your family. Few of my friends. You were little more than a secret that could be denied. There was flammable material in Burntcoat. Its name was fated; it had waited for this coronation. It plays again and again in my memory, that selfish desire.

A long time later I listened to a Spanish doctor speaking about his work in the critical-care units – one of the many retrospective programmes in the years that followed. He had the cast of an old sobered boxer. Speaking eloquently in English, he described the futility, the useless life support. After a while he shook his head and returned to Spanish. I remember the vivid images of the subtitles.

The bodies were smouldering around me, like embers in a pit. I was not in a hospital, not even in hell. I was sitting at the table playing cards with Death. For each of my patients, flip, flip. Mine, mine. As a doctor you cannot quit that casino. Sometimes Death felt sorry for me, or generous, or he didn't care and he let me win a few, randomly. That way the game continues.

I read the words and heard his voice crack and I broke down and ran along the river, until my lungs gave in. He knew. He knew exactly.

To talk of being haunted is not right; it describes something insubstantial, untouchable, which might be exorcised. It suggests an alternate world, terror seething in its own dimension or a hand passing through glass. Visitation. Not the collapsing human machine, the putrid, bluish organism being rendered down in the same room.

There was a moment it appeared the fever had broken. I heard the crackling of tarpaulin and came into the bedroom to find you sitting upright, your eyes focused, the delirium lifted.

Hey, how are you feeling?

Yes, you said.

You looked relaxed, strangely lambent. Your lips were thick with dead skin, but your hair was no longer damp. The face when pain has passed is utterly gorgeous; it's almost possible to think God created it.

Would you like some water?

Yes.

I made to leave.

Hülya nasıl?

Hülya?

What is our little one doing?

Relief swept through me. We were back to our game, our imaginary life.

She's colouring a butterfly and drinking milk.

Is she sick?

No – Halit. Of course not.

I looked at you. The smile was blissfully drawn; your eyes were glassy, their lenses glinting. Your fingers lifted and gently stroked the air.

I'll get the water. You must be so thirsty.

Teşekkürler, canım.

When I returned you were asleep again, the momentary bulb extinguished.

Your body argued on for another day, beyond the point of dehydration. It had lost its sheen and become chalk-like. Your throat seemed blocked, the spooned water spilled out. You needed intravenous fluid; I knew. I called for an ambulance. Several times I called the helpline, waited, pleaded for help. At The Anchorman the phone rang with no reply and Kendra's mobile was off. I went out on the street to find a soldier, someone in charge, a stranger, but the street was empty. It seemed impossible that any of it was happening.

There was the brittle snapping of air passing through your gullet. Your tongue was like wood. I tried to drip water in from a cloth but this time you started to choke; it felt like murder. I was beginning to feel ill too, vague in what I was doing, had forgotten to do. It was not just lack of sleep and exhaustion – there were sores on my hands, a band of pain around my brow. I lay on the floor in the bedroom doorway, where the rising smell didn't reach me, slept delusively, as if tending a newborn. Sometimes I was not sure if I was asleep or awake.

I didn't pray. I begged and shouted, but to no one, or at you. There are so many things I don't believe, though once I believed, so fiercely, that I would hold Naomi in my arms, warm until she was cold. In the end I did not even see her body. I shouted and then I was quiet, an observer.

It was night, or nearly dawn, the minutes hung between. I was turning the handle of the coffee grinder. The beans were tumbling and grating through the mill. I kept turning the handle, slowly, purposefully, like you'd shown me, full of dread that it was taking so long, unable to stop. I was out of my mind, I think, and hypnotised by the lustre and tarnish in the old brass casing. Perhaps you called to me, but I never heard. I could feel the strength of the virus, and its purpose. I started talking, making a transaction like a child trying to control the future.

When this is done it will all be over.

When this is done it will all be over.

I stopped the handle, transferred the powder to the pot, lit the stove and waited for the black liquid to rise. I sat and drank. Forgive me.

When I returned, the body was on its back, one hand on the stomach. Its head was tilted, the mouth was open and the eyes had a faint zincing on their surface. Grey-green skin, as if smoked. It radiated nothingness. The entire energy of the room had reversed.

I knelt on the plastic sheet and crawled to where the body lay. I moved the heavy arm and put my head against the wall of the chest, which was cool and silent as mud on the riverbank. Halit had gone and you had come. I let you hold me.

o

Our bones, our brains and nerves are so well constructed, our lives, ephemera; this is the contradiction, the impossible exchange. The government has apologised and made reparations. There have been mass suits, millions paid out. Like the miners, those poisoned by blood transfusions or incinerated in lethal towers, the damage is unquestionable. Though there was little control over the disease itself, and though the prime minister volunteered for the first vaccine two years later, the administration was obliterated, is known by its black watch.

After the recession, money was paid out to families, to survivors who would die of relapse. Sometimes the payments went into empty accounts. But there is no compensation. A wound to the psyche is incalculable. I can't say any mishandling mattered in the end. We catch the bus on time and the sinkhole still opens. We fly, and the white, forked tongue catches the aircraft. Our only right is to live in a true world.

The body remained in Burntcoat for several days. Long enough for the muscles to relax again, for the skin to marble, swell, for flies to begin to colonise. I was sick, my instincts were gone, but also I chose – not to let go. I wasn't afraid, not of that. I'd seen it on the moors. The foddering. Nature is anaerobic, amalgamated, and extraordinary only when sparked. I covered it with the tarpaulin but I kept looking, until the face became too different, no one I could recognise.

I sat nearby with a blanket and the room was empty and inhabited. I couldn't comprehend yet. Most of my life I'd been waiting; you'd been promised, you'd promised to come. There were so many ways to imagine, forms, cyphers, etched darkly in graveyards, blown in rings of smoke. But you were, you are, beyond imagination.

Eventually I got up. I drank a glass of water, then another. I looked at myself in the mirror, pale, smeared, obviously descending. I held the sink, fought the dizziness. The mirror seemed to shutter, its silver closing and opening, or the air behind me turned to show its hidden side, for just a moment.

I tried to gather myself, found my phone in the mess around the bed. The battery was flat so I plugged it in to charge, and when it switched on there was a message, sent from Halit in a half-lucid moment. An address.

The number he had written down and underlined after calling for medical advice was a registry and removal service. I was entering the serious rise of illness when I rang, could feel it beginning to infiltrate every system, my limbs, stomach, the thoughts strangely fluting inside my skull. There was a patch of light standing beside the window, filled with extraordinary, painful lumens, its nebula almost purple and green. You shed the dull skin coat. The line simply rang until it was answered. The operator asked to use my first name. I was calm, unusually detached. Perhaps he was used to hysteria, last-stage panic; he asked me several times.

Are you sure your partner has passed away?

His accent was familiar. I thought I even recognised the voice, someone from school. *Is your name Mark?*

There was a pause.

No. It's Ashley.

He spoke slowly, humanely stewarding, like an undertaker.

Edith, we ask if you could please ensure there is someone at the property until our arrival. We recommend you do not touch the body as it may pose a health hazard. We are very sorry for your loss, Edith.

I thought, they will come immediately, this hour. There could not be so many people waiting. After a while, I assumed they couldn't find the building. I waited by the studio door, wrapped in a blanket and swept by chills. Then I left the door standing open, came back upstairs, lay on the sofa and fell asleep. When I woke it was dark, my mouth tasted of soil and nausea rushed through me. I stumbled to the bathroom and was sick several times. I dragged myself back to the couch.

Their feet on the floorboards woke me. There were three of them in protective suits and visors, standing in the middle of the room, smooth, white, aliens. I sat up unsteadily, rose to my feet and staggered, then sat again – they did not approach. Two men and a woman; paramedics or army. The woman spoke.

Edith Harkness?

Yes.

You reported a death.

I pointed to the bedroom. The woman went in, and I lay back down, my head spinning. When she returned, no pronouncements were made; the state of the body was obvious. One of the men was carrying a small bag of portable equipment. He and the other went in, bagged it, carried it through the building and down the stairs. They were very quick or I had lost consciousness. The woman was standing beside me. I should cry, I thought, Halit deserves sorrow, but the thought itself was soporific. When I spoke, I made no sense.

Is it still here?

No. My colleagues have completed the removal.

It was in him.

Do you mean the virus? The body is still contagious. It will be handled accordingly.

I opened my eyes again. The white-suited woman was sitting on a chair at the table, writing a form. She asked questions I could barely answer. What was the name of the man? Was this his permanent residence? Did I have any identification for him?

Ms Harkness? Can you tell me who he was?

I pointed at the wallet on the table; she opened it, took out the cards.

Konstadin Konstadinov?

I shook my head, confused.

No.

She repeated the name on the card she was holding, and I remembered.

Yes.

She wrote the certificate, left a copy on the table.

The remains will be kept temporarily by the state. Do you understand what's happening, Ms Harkness?

She stared at me through the visor; her face clarified, became ageless.

Is there anyone that can help you?

Yes.

Please call them.

She stood, and left.

o

I was fortunate, though I can't say I am lucky. To live through the disease was to be in a current so strong and fast the landscape blurred, became unrecognisable. Parts of it I don't remember at all. The fever came fast, was swifter to peak. I pulled the tarpaulin off the bed and lay on the bare mattress. There was sickness and pain in every inch, every membrane. I woke on the floor, several times, once with my head bleeding profusely. I drank from the old water glasses, the tap, and I filled the sink like a trough. I broke things, shouldering them over, or I smashed them deliberately, in some mysterious violent psychosis – one of Jonah's photographs, too high on the wall to have been an accident. I left the refrigerator standing open, the ice trays scattered, and placed bloody tissues in a ring, like votives. To live through it was to be an animal in the river, half-drowned, lowing, caught against the few saving branches.

In the height of the fever you were with me. You were blindingly solid, covered by cloth that was soft as ash. You took my hand, leaned over me with a canine reek, and said, *Stay here.*

The otherness of that state. Like being born, feeling a first raw world, an infection soul-deep. I know I wanted Naomi, I heard myself calling for her; she had gone walking and was lost. She could not come back. You were in the cottage garden as I built the boat. You came up behind me and your arms wrapped like eels round my neck and belly, leeched my small bare chest. I wet myself, and the snow around my feet hissed. The sleep was restless and warping – dreams took me to infancy, to the building of the Witch, winching her up on chains above the gorse as the traffic roared past, to the restaurant door where someone I didn't know was working in the kitchen, to an old age I would never have, my skin wrinkled and slack. And I saw your face. At the summit, in the fit, when I was on fire and still alive, when I knew I would see the other side, you opened the mask. Behind it, appalling, extracting endlessness.

o

The world doesn't come back as it was before. The seas and mountains remain, the cities slowly fill up again, jets take off over ochre and turquoise aprons. Finance begins to move. Children are allowed to play together. Humanity is re-established. There is grief, its long cortège; the whole world joins and walks. Such shock is both disabling and enlivening; everything before was a mistake. We will do it differently; we'll repent. Consume less, conserve more, make sense of our punishment. It's been said the virus reached levels of superiority other pathogens never have. Like the vastation of ice ages, and condensed gene pools, language, blood and milk, it will evolve us. Of course, the old ways return. Our substance is the same; even with improving agents. We are our worst tendencies. We remain in our cast.

For days I could barely operate. Walking was a battle; I was reminded every few steps of the enormous damage, the point to which my body had been taken. White noise, on high and low frequencies, came and went. I lived off stale cereal and chocolate, whatever was left in the cupboards that I could get at; my hands were weak as petals. I lost so much mass that the joints in my shoulders looked like brackets. And I could hear every beat of my heart, a dull miracle I didn't believe.

I wasn't the last of a kind and I wasn't alone in the trauma of surviving. The outer levels are difficult to re-enter after such things. Patients lucky enough to be in hospital have spoken of feeling as if they were leaving monasteries when they were discharged. No one knew what to do with the terrible gift they'd been given – passports back home, albeit temporary. To sit in a cafe and drink tea, to pass other people close by in the street, brush against a stranger, kiss, all of it was transgressive.

I couldn't get past the door of Burntcoat. I could hardly talk to friends, and so many were also in shock. I thought of the safest places: the cedar forest behind the grandfather house, its roof luminescing at twilight, its immense trunks soundproofing the interior. The avenue up Mount Haguro – I imagined the stone steps leading through infinite trees, and thought, just one more, every day. My mother had done it, exercising her tongue, training the signals, repeating *I, I, I, am Na-o-mi*. Standing, unassisted. I waited with everyone else for the storm to pass, for rations and vitamins to be delivered, and sat and read about the world, its history, as if looking for proof.

It was not possible to stand before a mirror. I watched light wracking inside the frame, saw a shadow instead of my reflection and a sea of bright particles behind me, like an optical migraine. There was strobing opposite wherever mirrors hung. I felt soluble, draining towards the disrupted patch, atom by atom, and so I took all the mirrors down. To be inside a body is to assume its rim and edge, separation, to be trapped in an extraordinary vehicle, steering and thinking, regulating a thousand systems at once. I didn't know how. Or who I might be. I found myself online, all the profiles that said I existed. In the studio I took the bone from the throat of the wolf and held it, millions of years in my hands, and then I put it back.

When I emerged, the park grass was still tall and wild, like a meadow. Chaff was blowing across the streets and the leaves were already thinning, beginning to crisp and colour. The mornings were cool and I wrapped myself in a scarf and jumpers, underweight, and spent, after the strange aestivation. I practised walking to the end of the road and back, then further, along the river, into the centre of the city. I walked to Biraz. Its window was boarded up, a smoke-blackened frame around it. A stranger took hold of my arm and I realised I was weeping.

At first I wanted to deny it, to believe the problems were nerve damage, or the aftermath of trauma. There were momentary losses of perception, and the visual and auditory disturbances came regularly. They were hard to describe to the doctor. Dark and light constituents flushing together and apart, bands, currents. It might be on the periphery, folds in the corner of my eye. Or I would look up and see it directly ahead, a colourless aurora, sometimes with the corona of red and green. The sounds, even if above or below my register of hearing, still affected my body. My skin and the hairs on my limbs responded as if swept. The waves penetrated me, passed through with no resistance. Other times there was just a steady static monologue.

I was told it would resolve as I got better, but it didn't. I began sleeping in the studio, as I had done before the building was renovated, on a makeshift bed – the largest space, where nothing felt close. On bad days I wore the Peltors I used when operating the compressor and lathe. My eyes and ears were tested. The results were normal. The doctor prescribed tinted glasses with large wraparound lenses, and ambient music at night, then diagnosed PTSD and suggested therapy. Victims of the virus were suffering all kinds of physical and psychological effects, he said. Dozens of aftercare programmes were being set up. I agreed to a referral. I spoke to a psychologist, then another.

It's as if there's something there. The texture is different. There's energy.

It must be very frightening, Edith. Would you describe yourself as quite sensory? Are you affected by disharmonic noise and things like different material? Cotton wool or aluminium foil?

Not really. Isn't everyone?

These were the symptoms of a paranoiac. But I wasn't that.

The layers were peeled back as I talked. It all made sense, the therapist said. The core of my childhood was pessimistic. To be robbed of a partner only reinforces the notion. In the past year, we had all seen diabolic things and felt the presence of death. The preoccupation was normal, and should be mindfully dealt with. I was encouraged to think I'd made you, that in my childhood you were the defining fear, the expectation – my perspective had been set by it, like a painting's ghost pavement. Every day, I lived by that principle; absorbed the idea. To reduce fear, I was asked to draw your face, give you substance. As if the entire history of art hadn't already failed.

Once I felt stronger I began to work in small ways again, sketching, using the kiln, which was slower and less violent than the blowtorches. I finished the commission. It felt like work from another era, a reproduction of work by a different artist.

I spoke with Karolina, told her, in part, what had happened. She'd left many concerned messages. She was used to long silences from me, months during which I would disappear into a project. The conversation was emotional and halting. She was uncustomarily flustered and I was unused to pastoral care. She could come, she said – that very day, if I needed her to. If I was not ready for visitors she could have anything sent, arrange private medical treatment, physiotherapy if I needed it.

I'm all right, I told her. *Getting better.*

Darling, I am so glad.

Her voice broke. Several clients had died, and colleagues, her elderly mother in France, whom she had not had the chance to see or say goodbye to. Into the void, more and more names fell. I told her I was sorry and when I said it I saw Halit's eyes, their pale fire extinguished.

En avant toute. En avant toute.

She steered to business, described the decimation of the arts.

I suspect things will be quite difficult for some time. What shall I tell the trust?

Tell them the piece is done. They can arrange transport.

Some department of the government informed Halit's family. I was thankful not to have that task. I did not apply to retrieve his remains; a body belongs to the mother who creates it. The other obligation was unavoidable. I boxed his possessions – the boots, old, polished, with new laces inserted, shirts that I carefully laundered and folded, his books and phone, his soft leather wallet. I did not know what they would want. I wrote a letter. The translation app scrambled the sentences and the sentiment became

191

lost, so I wrote in English, hoped a member of the family might be able to decipher it. The letter was extremely painful. I described us as friends, not wanting to offend anyone.

I was privileged to know Halit. He was a kind, gentle man of real integrity. He made me laugh. Through him my world . . .

All of this was true, but underneath the respectful words the relationship was clear.

I sent the box to the address Halit had given me. I kept the brass coffee grinder – the only real heirloom, perhaps, and an outright theft. I told myself he had no children, no genuine inheritors; we were much more than just lovers. If he had lived . . . Feeble justification. The truth was I could not let it go. I don't use it, hardly ever, but I've kept it all these years on the same shelf. It stands elegantly in its Ottoman casing, glints dully like the key to a huge gate.

I didn't expect anyone to call. When the number came up with a code I did not recognise, I almost didn't answer. There was a pause before a man began talking. His voice sounded set back from the microphone, as if the call was on speaker.

Hello. Hello. Can I speak to Edith?

The accent was thick, his words unpractised. A few sentences learnt for the purpose of the call.

Yes. Who is this, please?
I am Deniz Öztürk.

When I realised it was Halit's father, I began to talk, too fast, nervously. He didn't understand. Halit had told me about them, I said, stories from when he was a boy, the cherry tree in the garden, the earthquake. I heard rapid discussion, someone else speaking in the background, telling his father what I had said. He waited, then asked, or perhaps read out, his questions. Was I with Halit in the hospital? Did he talk of his family? Was there suffering? The last question with its fist inside the man's heart. I was honest, and said what I could. I felt the air warp and pulse. You were beside me in the room, as an adult might stand next to a child who needs assistance, who might lie without meaning to. Yes, I was his girlfriend, not for very long, half a year. We were locked in together. The sickness was bad. I did what I could.

It was disquieting, the sudden materialisation of Halit through others, those far more qualified and entitled. I heard the translation given, then I heard a woman cry out, her moan of anguish, unbridled weeping. Deniz Öztürk came back on the line. His voice was hoarse, the voice of a labourer, a folk musician, the bereaved.

We want to say thank you, Edith.
No, I said. *No, I am not to be thanked.*

Yes, he insisted. *Thank you.*

I fought back tears. I remembered what to say.

Üzgünüm.

There was a long silence; neither of us knew how to break the connection. I hung up.

I took the canoe out on the river, paddled down to The Anchorman and held the garden rail. Kendra and Nick had both been ill, and Nick was being rehabilitated. They had lost their daughter. Three years and seven years – their markers for relapse. I would sit with Kendra in the hospice and hold her hand and think, when it is my turn I will not be in here.

There was a yellow notice stuck to the door of the bar. The building lay dark and empty inside, looked culpable, as if it had been, all along, a crime scene of some kind. As if our need for society was dangerous.

o

The second half of my life, everything since, has been downstream. I've made different choices, tried to make amends. I don't drive. I don't eat meat. I am careful not to waste. When I travelled, it was offset. I didn't join any church, or the nova parties. I didn't enlist in trials or pay premium insurance. I've taken care of myself, though not in order to prolong anything. There's no reason why I should have been spared. Genetic coils, a biological oversight. Or imitation, acceptance; I was taught by an expert. Sometimes, though I'm encouraged not to, I think, it's because you sensed in me a good partner, a millionth wife, who is loyal, who makes effigies in your honour, creates enough intrigue to see dawn break, and then another.

I've let go of things – not in any spiritual sense, though I like those doctrines. We must learn loss, not as a beginner but as a ready player. There have been lovers since. Not many. One was my assistant and I can't say I didn't care for him. I could have been a mother – there are ways to protect the foetus, inhibitors. But I was already defined, betraying some cause each time I imagined a different passage. You were my only certainty.

I sold Naomi's archive. Her work came back into fashion; she was exhumed from the burial site of forgotten writers. Of course, she'd also produced a daughter of merit. They've reassessed her writing, the label of Gothic stripped off like cheap varnish. Karolina once said to me the term is used for women whose work the establishment enjoys but doesn't respect. Men are the existentialists. There was increasing interest in her papers from American establishments, and in the end I accepted an offer.

Naomi's archive contains the huge hospital file, its reams of notes and progress reports, the scans and surgical remarks. An unworn medical helmet. Drafts of her books – first on Croxley, neat, organised, then the baking paper, torn off at the edges and strangely parchment-like. There are gnomic instructions to herself and rehabilitation worksheets, her teaching notes and payslips. Pictures I drew for her that she kept – the emotion guides and notes of complaint.

I do not like curry in my beans, it gives me a hot tummy ache.

You hurt my feelings when you did not say well done for remembering my lines in the nativity or clap.

There's a photograph of her and me on the fells, beside the lower pools. Her face is impassive, and I seem to be roaring. We look unkempt, rustic, like bush-dwellers. I can't remember posing, or anyone taking the picture. Jonah would say, it's spirit photography, one of us took the picture and later appeared in the absent spot.

Not that I believe in that shit.

Now the archive is studied by writers and by neurologists. Naomi's cottage is used for residencies and has been connected to the national grid.

Several documents I incinerated. The court papers, including my father's custody statements, in which Naomi is depicted as a cold, hopeless mother, even before the haemorrhage. She did not breastfeed long enough, he said. She put me in a washing basket in the garden as a baby while she was writing, and a cat urinated on me and I caught toxoplasmosis. If I was left with her, I would be in danger, and irreparably damaged. I did not burn them to protect her. I did not do it to spare him. Between evidence and illusion, we are all located.

A few years after the pandemic, a man called Erik contacted me to tell me our father had died. He was my half-brother, six years younger. He was sorry to inform me of the news. It was cancer, stage IV, very rapid; Adam had received excellent medical care. Erik apologised that I had not had the opportunity to visit or say goodbye. There was a photograph of his family in the letter, his partner and a child, Erik standing with his hands round their shoulders, and a handsome woman, in her fifties, all of them smiling and suntanned. I had been dimly aware of my relatives in Canada: siblings, nieces and nephews, a woman who, under a different alignment, could have been my stepmother. I tried to see in Erik aspects I recognised, the long nose, the fine eyebrows.

We began emailing each other. He knew very little about his father's first marriage and I did not go into detail. The stories he told did not correspond with the man I remembered. Adam had gone to another country and put on a different character, like a casual jacket. Halit had spoken about this too – the urge to migrate is the urge to escape and create, not recreate. I sensed in Erik's letters some kind of investigation into himself, alongside the responsibility of rounding up a lost member of the herd. He was curious about me, though his sister Tabby was hesitant. She'd been their father's favourite, Erik said – but she would come round eventually.

He visited England on business and we arranged to meet. I took the train to the capital. Erik met me at the station; we shook hands, and he kept hold of mine.

Oh my God, it's so strange, it's really great. Isn't it?

We spent an awkward but pleasant enough after-noon walking around the sites. His questions were straightforward, easy to answer, his cheerfulness of a different order. He wanted to talk about his father, the grief having entered a milder, reconciled stage. He didn't want to unearth painful truths, just to reassure himself, and address the mysteries, confirm an ability to metabolise the difficult aspect.

I took him into the foyer of the Honing Trust, showed him The Conundrum. I made a joke about foyer art being the death of an artist, but he didn't understand.

Oh, wow. This is beautiful, Edith. You're very talented. He did talk a lot about your art.

Did he?

I'd love to know more about this, Erik said.

It gave me quite a bit of trouble. Well, the wolf was cooperative.

I described the processes, our native trees. The bird's long, narrow beak was entering the throat as precisely as a surgical instrument, its head surrounded by teeth. The wolf's claws were lying next to the crane's foot, interlinking. It was unsettling, seeing the piece again. I wanted to leave and Erik misinterpreted.

You're very humble, Edith.

I'm really not. Just like to move on.

I must have seemed almost exactly what he suspected me to be: intense, unpacked, a person made from a radically different set of circumstances. He said as much.

We are chalk and cheese. Is that the right expression? Dad used to say it.

Yes, that's right.

There was a pause.

I guess he didn't always do such a good job.

I glanced at him; he was looking at the installation.

Did you forgive him?

It's not something I've thought much about.

We talked for a while about reforestation in Canada, his daughter. He was generous.

She looks like her mom, but now I see you there's something too. Next time I should bring her and Kate. Or you could come visit us. In summer we have a place on the lake.

I didn't tell him I'd been to Canada several times. We talked of the virus, which was still at the fore of all conversations, like a gigantic astral event, a ruinous deity that had visited Earth. Canada had been less badly affected than other nations; there'd been space, better policies, of course.

Erik opened doors, was meticulously considerate. The courtesy I thought at first might relate to having a sister began to seem like a gentle form of pity. I was the orphan, the outlier, no matter how successful I'd become. Over beer, when his courage was up, he asked, was it an interesting childhood? The question was unintentionally prejudiced.

Very, I said. *We lived sort of at the edge.*

There was no point in undoing the tie, the fear of the unknown.

My sister is a little competitive, he said. *She's used to being the boss. I don't think she likes the idea of a famous big sister.*

Well, I'm clearly not that.

He shrugged.

She's smart. She knows who not to go up against.

I walked him to his hotel, and he hugged me to his chest. His cologne was resinous, agar, faint and lost on his large frame. He seemed full of emotion and relief.

Edith, it was so good to finally meet you.

Afterwards, I saw Karolina in her club – an old-fashioned townhouse with a starred restaurant below. She ordered champagne as if it were an occasion: I was an infrequent guest there, had always felt uneasy, like a stray mongrel. It was still hard for me to be with people, and I found myself caring far less whether I conveyed it. The club had kept going, illegally, during confinement. The penalty was huge, but some politically connected members had saved it from being closed down.

Did you come here? I asked Karolina.

Absolutely not. It was idiotic. I did not leave the house once.

There were one or two celebrities at other tables, and an industry patron – minister for the arts – who wanted to speak with me. The introduction was brief; we'd met previously, before his party's election to office. Sir Philip had the decency to ask for the table to be cleared of champagne glasses. The commission was broached and I was asked to create a national memorial. For the million who had died, and, he did not say it directly, those who still would. It was beginning to be understood that the disease was incurable and the population was divided – those who'd escaped and had since been vaccinated, and those for whom it was too late. He knew, if I would pardon the intrusion into my personal life, that I had experienced AG3. I stared at his suit, at the tie of inordinately beautiful olive silk. It's in such moments we realise how minimal our experiences are, how slight our qualification to represent. No budget was discussed. There was no mention of contingency. Nothing was being put out to tender. I shook Sir Philip's hand, thanked him for the esteem with which he regarded my work.

Take a while to think about it, Karolina said, after he left. *They will wait.*

That's not sensible.

I told Karolina what I'd been doing that day, described my new brother, the incongruity. It was a good story, a confession of sorts. She was intrigued by the development.

Is he similar at all? What does he do?

Banking. I think I confused him.

I'm certain you did.

Her hair was set in its neat French braid, grey woven in thoroughly. Across her throat was the trickle of fine gold chain and hollow orb she always wore. She chastised the man at the next table for taking out his phone. She was growing undeniable with age and softening towards those in her keep. No one was unchanged.

I was beginning to feel uncomfortable, the background talk and music, and asked if we could walk to a park or the gardens next to the agency, a quiet space. The streets of the capital were as they had always been, thronging with bodies, frenetic, a lottery of faces. I put on the coloured glasses and light filtered through lilac, the spectrum moderated. The buildings relaxed against each other. A trick of control, to calm stress, but sometimes it seemed to work.

Karolina took my arm, wove me between pedestrians and buses, and talked as we walked.

I've known several men who have attempted a family, failed dreadfully, then repeated it with more success. A teacher, my music teacher actually, she was a very beautiful tragic person, once said to me, the job of a woman is to improve a man for the next woman.

That's depressing, I said. What about the previous one?

She learns too, of course. If she's wise, she chooses herself next time. Do you think it's true?

Yes, maybe. What happened to your teacher?

Oh, I disappointed her. I stopped singing.

We sat in the private garden. It was warm; the cherry tree in the middle of the lawn was flowering. The meeting with my brother had left me disconcerted. I'd felt somehow returned to the margin while his sense of belonging had been reinforced.

What did you think of my mother? I asked Karolina. *I know she was represented by Alexander Saul, I know you liked her work, but you talked to her?*

I did. I met her here, at a party.

Did you like her?

She regarded me for a moment with a gambler's dead eye, decided to lay a card.

We had an argument. About children. She called me a bitch for suggesting she should have left the baby at home in order to circulate.

What? I was there?

Yes, in a sling. You were extremely loud. Your napkin needed changing. I'd just joined Saul and babies were not supposed to be on the agenda.

Karolina laughed, delighted.

It was the way she said it, almost compassionately, as if she were helping me. 'Is there really any need to be a bitch to another woman?'

That's like something she might have said after the surgery.

Is it? It seemed a very natural question. And important, don't you think? I've thought about it a lot. How would you have answered, Edith?

I don't really understand the concept.

Of a bitch?

Of a woman.

Karolina laughed again.

Yes, she said. *Just to warn you, if you accept Sir Philip's offer, you may well end up on the honours list.*

I don't think I can do it.

Of course not. But who can?

Karolina had invited me to stay with her, but I took the sleeper train home, dozed in the big seat as it ran at reduced speed through night-lit towns, faster in the liminal spaces between. I disembarked with the other northern exiles and walked back to Burntcoat along the river, in the early, alkaline light.

o

The orange tree is full of white flowers – this room is filled with the smell. After the fall I got myself up, packed soil back around the roots and dragged the pot close to the bed. I sat by the window, slept, then looked at the river, imagining a structure built above the water, diving or rising seamlessly. I ate a few almonds to keep the nausea away – a trick I learnt from Subhadassi – and tried to sketch for a while. My drafting is very bad; I can't make my hand cooperate and concentrating is getting harder.

The self-pity has passed, or at least it's put away. I have to rest continually now, which is itself a commitment, exertion of sorts.

The tree's scent is so insistent. Halit emerges from it as if through a doorway, walking up the iron steps of the fire escape, a wing tip brushing the wall. If I turn round, his image will be beautiful, or he will appear terrifying, foul and dark as my heart. The messenger comes as I am – that's what is written in Scriptures. I read them afterwards, curious, and disappointed. The solipsism of humans, even in imagining our end. The clues we give ourselves that we are self-made, while disowning our maker, our chaos and art.

Halit, pushing me to the ground, or me pulling him down. Afterwards we lie with our mess, our fragrance. And the citrus blossom is cologne to receive you, as you follow him – the lip of a great vortex, the true abstract, finally arriving for me.

In the studio, in the nova piece, I've described both you and he, and a coital woman, her arms reaching up, ecstatic, complicit. She's prehistoric oak, tannicly preserved, unearthed from the wetlands in the east. She has a lover with two faces behind her. One is impossible, scorched and tarred, made of rotoring blades that will funnel the wind and rain towards its twin, hastening first his decay, then hers. The other is the face of a man I loved briefly, for ever. Forms joined and hollow, containing no soul except air. I can't imagine it's what they want. It cannot possibly comfort, or reparate.

There's no title, and I could not bring myself to sign the plinth. My name is engraved on one of the steps of the memorial ascent, along with all the other surnames – Sean's idea. Always the stonemason. He's arriving tomorrow to collect the piece. He has keys to the yard and outer door. I won't be needed.

I remember this tiredness, the sheer weight of it. I'm beginning to feel chilled, by every small movement. I'll keep the stove going while I can. I know what to expect, at which point to stop it. Before the acute stage, when I'm turned inside out and can't swallow. Before the fever robs all sense. There's a jug of water beside the bed, boxes of pills. Is that cowardice? I'm just trying to proceed without suffering and distress, execute a choice. I'm trying not to look away, to accept my form tending towards its new state, carbon matter, microbes, the flesh expanding and shrinking, beginning to decay.

But you want to test my mettle. You want me to confront it with no defence. Like that small child who walked into the hospital room alone, to see the unutterable, riven mark left by your near miss. They say you're not here, that I should think of you impersonally, or not at all. I know what you are.

These open sections of air don't disappear any more. The room keeps destructing, letting me see behind – that infinite, unlit substance. The sound in my ears is like screaming in the falling car. And I remember exactly my dying dream, your face and the force of its maw, being eviscerated by it, every fibre in me resisting, holding on.

I won't win, won't survive.

But my mind tightens its grip. My body can't help fighting, can't change its instinct – cells crawling along the blood's hot walls to save it. Once, when Naomi was gone all day, I swam to the bottom of the biggest pool, under the waterfall, where everything was blind silt and the stasis was like the cold muscle of space. There was no surface, no air, and the panic was atomic, brought me back up with such explosive power.

I want to sit with Naomi again.

I want to say to Shun, yes, of course, I'm the wood in the fire. I've experienced, altered in nature. I am burnt, damaged, more resilient. A life is a bead of water on the black surface, so frail, so strong, its world incredibly held.

Acknowledgements

I am extremely grateful to The Royal Literary Fund and The Society of Authors' Contingency Fund for supporting grants in 2019 and 2020.

Thanks to the following editors and readers for enduring feverish versions of this novel: Alex Bowler, Kate Nintzel, Tracy Bohan, Peter Hobbs, Jennifer Custer, Jin Auh and Dr Richard Thwaites. Thanks to Silvia Crompton for copy-editing.

I greatly appreciate the guidance with scientific, cultural and artistic research from the following people: Sarah Munro, Director at the BALTIC Centre for Contemporary Art; Polly Roy OBE, Professor of Virology at the London School of Hygiene & Tropical Medicine; Imogen Cloët, Russ Coleman, Hamit Sert, Ayumi White, Damon Galgut, Lenny Benterman, Jonathan Hall and Lila Azam Zanganeh.

My heartfelt thanks to the following extraordinary women for their support during this extraordinary year: Chloe Manka, Johanna Forster, Morgan Pickard, Louise Cole, Kelly Smith, Rowan Pelling, Jane Kotapish, Fiona Renkin, Joanna Härmä, Rebecca Watts, Naomi Wood, Sarah Perry, Julie de Ruiter, and Lila and Imogen again.

Love and gratitude to my dad, who was always there, and to my darling Loy, so full of joy, courage and kindness.